Pierced

Love like Yours, Book #2

NICOLE S. GOODIN

Pierced
Love like Yours Series – Book #2
Published by Nicole S. Goodin

ISBN: 9780473396961

I would like to dedicate this to every person who took a chance and spent their time reading Rushed. You're all stars and I thank you from the bottom of my heart for your support and encouragement.

Pierced is book #2 in the Love like Yours Series.
It is a novella, tying up some of the loose ends for Ellerslie and Lawson, and opening the door to Quinn's future.
I hope you enjoy reading it as much as I enjoyed writing it.
Nicole x

Prologue

Lawson

It was strange to think that such a short time ago it was just me... and then I found El... or maybe she found me – and I had something I never even knew I was looking for.

I thought I had everything.

As per usual, life had other plans.

One event would alter our entire course...

We hadn't even made it down the aisle yet, and already there was a baby in the picture. I knew she was going to turn my whole fucking life upside down. How I would run a business, care for a family and still cherish El... I had no clue.

I wasn't sure I had what it took to be a good father, I knew Ells would be a great mother, and Aunty Quinn had promised she would be there to help in any way we needed.

I was determined to try my hardest. I wanted to be the best I could be for her when she arrived. She was part of my family... her, El and I... we were a family now.

If I was really being honest with myself, just being a new father was not my main concern – learning to be a father to a child that wasn't mine? Yeah... that was up there on the list.

"Someday, someone might come into your life and love you the way you've always wanted."
- Author unknown

1. Lawson

Six months...

I had six more long months until she was my wife. It had already been three months since the day I'd proposed, and every single day I'd had to wage the war within myself, to drag her away and make her mine immediately.

It was going to be a bloody long six months.

El and I, mainly El, were planning a small ceremony for our closest family and friends. We had been to Jemma and Connor's wedding reception a month ago and it was absolute chaos. I think they carried a bit of guilt for everyone missing their quickie Vegas wedding, so they'd invited *absolutely* everyone they knew and had a huge party. It was a great night, but it wasn't mine or El's style. We were going for small and intimate.

The truth was, I would have given her whatever she wanted. I just wanted the day to be perfect for her. If she'd wanted a big wedding, then she would have gotten one. Thankfully, she hadn't been the least bit interested.

Just another reason I love that woman.

I glanced at the calendar on my desk. October fifth. Tomorrow was my thirty-third birthday. El hadn't said a word about it. I knew her well enough to know she was up to something, but I also knew her well enough to know that she liked to surprise me, so I hadn't asked a single question about what she was planning.

I packed up my desk, flicked off the lights and headed up to El's floor.

The favorite part of my work day.

I was the luckiest bastard in this building – I knew it, and so did everyone else. Ellerslie was as rare as a unicorn. Smart, sweet, kind, beautiful...

God, she's so beautiful.

Six more months...

It was getting late for a Friday evening, and West had gone home. I knocked on her door and waited before entering, just in case she was in a late phone meeting.

"Come in," she called out in her sweet voice. Just hearing the sound had my heart beating faster.

She was sitting at her desk, busy as usual. I couldn't even begin to imagine how she managed to get through the amount of work that passed over her desk. Her workload put mine to shame.

"Hey, pretty girl." I went straight to her and kissed her on the forehead.

"Hey, cowboy." She pulled me back in for a quick peck on the lips. "Thanks for waiting for me. I'm sorry I'm taking so long, I'm just snowed under." She grabbed my hand and gave it a grateful squeeze. The zing of energy that raced up my arm still took me by surprise, even after all these months with her.

"No worries, I was busy too," I lied. I'd actually done sweet fuck all for the last hour and a half, but I knew how busy she was, so I'd waited.

"I'm about done now anyway. Is Quinn still in?" she asked as she typed.

"I'll check," I told her as I dropped my bag into a spare seat. I walked out the door and down the hall to my sister's office. I knocked loudly on the door and heard rustling and whispering from inside.

"Q? Are you in there?" I called as I knocked again.

"Just a minute," she yelled back.

I frowned. I could hear her giggling like a school girl in there. The door opened a crack.

"Hey, Law, ah... did you want something?" Q was a mess, her clothes were in disarray and she was all flustered.

Oh, you little shit...

"Yeah, I thought I might come in and have a coffee with you while I wait for El," I told her, ignoring the noise I could still hear behind her.

"Now isn't really a good time sorry, I'm just kinda busy."

Oh, I bet you are.

"Okay, no worries. I guess I'll see you tomorrow," I said as I turned to walk away. I grinned to myself "Catch ya later, Colt," I called out before she'd had a chance to close the door.

"See ya, man," I heard Colt call back just as Quinn pushed the door shut.

"For god sakes, I told you to be quiet," Quinn's muffled voice came from behind the door.

I chuckled and left them alone.

So much for not seeing him anymore...

I went back to El's office; she was still sitting at her desk, clicking away on her laptop. She was twirling a strand of long blonde hair around her finger as she worked. She startled as she noticed me watching her and a smile appeared on her full lips.

"Was she there?" she asked as she closed down her laptop and slid it into her bag.

I walked over and took it from her. "Oh yeah, she was there alright." I chuckled.

El looked at me quizzically. "So... did she want a ride home?"

I shook my head and chuckled again. "Nah, baby, I don't think she's quite finished in there yet."

El raised one eyebrow at me and waited.

"She's got company... if you know what I mean?"

El gaped. "Who? Not Colt?"

"Yeap," I replied, popping the p.

"*No way.*" She shook her head in disbelief. "She said she was finished with him." I shrugged. "I'm guessing that didn't go quite to plan."

El rolled her eyes. "Those two are useless. Someone's gonna get hurt."

"Quinn's a big girl. She'll be fine," I told her as we walked towards the elevators.

"It's not Q I'm concerned about," she muttered.

She was right. Colt was in way over his head with my sister. I knew Quinn had tried to stop seeing him a couple of times in the last few months, but he always seemed to claw his way back in. I had to give it to the guy; he was persistent when he wanted something.

We rode the elevator down to the car park, I opened El's door for her – she was finally getting used to it, and put our bags in the back seat of the truck. I loved that nearly every day I got to drive my girl to work and home again after. I still had to steady my breathing sometimes when I thought about it being our home. I could imagine us there together for many, many years. I could imagine us having our children there.

"When do you want to have a family?" I asked El suddenly.

She stopped singing and snapped her head around to look at me. "A family?" she asked in a squeaky voice.

"Yeah." I tapped the steering wheel nervously. "A family. You want one, right?"

Why the hell have we never talked about this before?

I'd never been overly concerned about having children. My life had always been career driven, but since I'd met El, everything was different. I wanted children with her more than just about anything in the world. I wanted to watch her stomach grow, I wanted to see her hold our baby for the first time... I couldn't wait to navigate our way through parenting together.

"Of course I do," she breathed. "I just didn't realize it was on your radar." She reached out for my hand and entwined our fingers. "When do *you* want to have a family?"

"Whenever you're ready," I told her with certainty. "We could start trying as soon as we get home if you want?" I grinned at her.

She squeezed my hand and laughed at my teasing. "I'm not sure that I'm ready to share you just yet... can we have this conversation again after the wedding?" she asked shyly.

"Sure, baby." I pulled her hand towards me and kissed it softly. "We'll just keep practicing until then."

***

I yawned as I woke. It had been a long night of practicing indeed. I stretched out, searching for El, but I came up empty-handed. Her side of the bed was cold. I glanced at the clock on my bedside.

7.20am.

El was definitely up to something, she never got up this early on a Saturday morning.

"El?" I called out.

Silence.

"El?" I tried again, more loudly – still no answer. I threw on a pair of sweats and went downstairs to look for her. Ellerslie wasn't there, neither was Zef. Now I was confused. Her Jeep was still parked in the garage, but her trainers were gone.

She's gone for a walk?

I smirked to myself. I was getting years of credit for this one... El had forgotten my birthday.

I went back upstairs to shower and dress for the day. If I was honest, I was a little disappointed. The best part of my day was waking up next to her, and I'd been sure she had something planned for today. My instincts were losing their touch.

I heard El the minute I shut the shower off. I rubbed the towel quickly through my hair and wrapped it around my waist. She was in the bedroom singing softly along to Ed Sheeran's 'Photograph'. I paused in the doorway to listen. I knew she'd stop as soon as she saw me. El didn't think she could sing. She wasn't wrong about much, but she was dead wrong about that. She had a beautiful voice.

She stopped singing, and I heard her rummaging around in a drawer. "Are you coming out of there today, birthday boy?" she called out to me. I could tell by the way her voice sounded that she was sporting a huge smile.

I couldn't help the grin that spread across my face as I stepped into the bedroom. My eyes landed on her immediately; she was stripped down to her underwear. Her sports bra was light blue and made her eyes look even bluer than usual. I'd barely glanced at her, but her sexy-as-fuck curves already had me hard.

"Happy birthday, handsome." Her voice caught as she saw me standing there, nearly naked.

We both stood still, not saying a word, just appreciating one another from afar. It didn't seem to matter how often I had her, I could never get enough. El didn't seem to be able to resist me when I was shirtless, so that was pretty much how I rolled these days. I watched her trace the lines of my tattoo with her eyes and then lick her lips.

I lost it.

I strode towards her and scooped her up under her perky ass. She shrieked as I chucked her onto the bed. "I want to unwrap my present," I growled in between placing kisses on her neck and jaw.

"Your present is downstairs." Her voice was a borderline moan.

"My present is right here." I unsnapped the front of her sports bra as I spoke.

Her breasts sprang free and this time she did moan. "Lawson."

I rolled onto my back and pulled her with me so she was straddling me.

Her big blue eyes were sparkling as she looked down at me. "You are so fucking hot," she panted. She rose up and tugged my towel so it opened loosely around my hips. She made an appreciative noise that sounded like a purr.

"Fuck, baby. I need you." I tugged her down to me and sighed in contentment at the feeling of her skin on mine, she was so soft, so warm. She fit perfectly against my big body.

She wiggled her hips against my erection and moaned again. "I want you now," she whispered as she began to shimmy her underwear down her legs. I couldn't take my eyes off her. Her breasts were bouncing in my face, her hips grinding against mine.

God, she's so sexy.

"Ride me," I commanded in a voice I knew she wouldn't argue with. El loved it as much as I did when I was in charge. It strengthened our trust – our bond.

I grabbed my dick in my hand, I knew El was ready, she was so wet. She hovered above me and slid down slowly, taking me in all the way to the base.

"Oh god," she whimpered as she slowly moved side to side, adjusting to the fullness.

I pushed my hips up and thrust into her gently. Fuck she felt so good. Sex without a condom was about the best feeling in the world.

El began to grind on me, rocking backwards and forwards. She looked so sexy sitting up on me, her breasts bouncing with every pump of her hips. I knew she was close already, I could feel the tremors beginning to race through her body, El was a grinder, she knew exactly how to get the right amount of friction, it never took long when she was in control.

Seeing her get off was the biggest turn on for me. Knowing that our bodies together gave her that pleasure.

Fuck...

She quickened her pace.

"Come for me, Ellerslie." Authority rang clear in my voice. I watched her tip over the edge, she fell forward onto my chest, shuddering and moaning.

I thrust up into her rapidly, and she cried out my name, "Lawson, oh fuck."

I flipped her in one motion onto her back and took control. I drove into her without mercy, my pace fierce and dominating. El was completely gone; she was a shuddering, writhing ball of nerves beneath me. "Now, baby," I choked out as

I chased my release to the end. I spurted hot and hard inside of her, claiming her again, in the most primal way. I rode it out until her body stilled underneath me and I felt her muscles relax.

"Oh god," El whispered as she ran a hand softly through my hair. "That was... wow."

I chuckled and kissed her nose. "That was something alright. I should have a birthday more often."

"Happy birthday, Lawson," she told me softly as she looked deep into my eyes. She saw me for exactly what I was, and loved me because of it.

"I love you."

"I love you more," she whispered as she leaned up to kiss my lips. I met her halfway and kissed her softly, sweetly – a complete contrast to the moment prior.

"Marry me," I insisted.

She waved her left hand, the one wearing my ring. "I think I remember agreeing to that already," she teased.

"Today... marry me today." I kissed her again.

She just giggled against my lips.

I sighed in defeat and hoisted her up into my arms. I carried her to the bathroom to join her for my second shower of the day.

2. Ellerslie

I smiled as I threw on some leggings and a long navy blue knit dress. Lawson was constantly on my mind, dominating my thoughts. The man didn't know how to do anything by halves. He was always all in. Shivers raced up my spine.

He's all in with me.

The quote he'd sent me a few days ago ran through my mind.

"If you're going to love someone or something then don't be a slow leaking faucet – be a hurricane." – Shannon L. Alder.

He didn't love quietly, or softly. Lawson loved me like a raging bull... he loved me like a hurricane.

I checked he was still in the bathroom before I raced downstairs to make sure I had everything set up the way I wanted it.

"Sit," I told Zef. He sat immediately – all those classes we'd taken him to were really paying off.

I tore out of the room and hid behind the door in the hallway to wait for him.

A few minutes passed before he came downstairs.

"Hey, boy." I heard Lawson walk into the room towards his dog. I heard the tinkle of Zefer's collar as he gave him a pat.

I waited patiently.

I heard him chuckle, he'd found the note.

I couldn't hold back a smile as I imagined him reading the words.

"I hope you don't mind, but I brought a friend to your party."

"El?" he called out in a concerned voice. "What friend, pretty girl? What party?"

I peaked my head around the door and got caught by his piercing eyes. I stepped out, pulling the lead gently behind me.

Lawson's eyes followed the lead down behind my back until they landed on the tiny puppy sitting on the floor.

"Happy birthday," I squeaked. Fuck, I was so nervous.

What if he hates it...

His eyes widened as he pointed at the puppy. "Is that ours?" he asked.

"He," I corrected him. "He is ours – well yours, it's *your* birthday." I rubbed my hands together nervously. I couldn't get a read on Lawson, it was unnerving. I screwed up my nose. "I might have already named him though..."

Fuck! What if he doesn't want a puppy?

Lawson had taken a few steps towards me and now he crouched down with his hand slowly extended towards the dog. "What's his name?" he asked without looking at me.

"Frank."

"Frank?" he asked, humor in his voice. "You gave our puppy an old-man name?"

Our puppy...

I snorted. "I think it's funny."

Lawson petted the puppy's head. "Do you think it's funny, Frank? Huh?"

Frank, having heard the name I'd spent several hours teaching him, perked up and jumped playfully at Lawson and licked his hand.

"Where did you get him?" he asked as he picked him up.

"As in right now?" I asked with my head cocked to the side.

God, they were so cute together.

Lawson nodded. "And where did you buy him?"

I grinned. "I've had him stashed at Quinn and Logan's for about five nights. That's where me and Zef snuck off to this morning."

Lawson chuckled. "I bet Q loved that."

I waved my hand at him. "She'll get over it; it was just *one* pair of heels."

Lawson's loud laugh moved through my body. I loved hearing him laugh. He tilted his head towards Zef. "Have they met?"

I nodded. "They sure have. I've had Frank going to day care with him all week." We'd had Zef booked into a dog day care for the past few months. He went there most days while we both were at work.

I called Zef over and took the lead off Frank. Lawson put him down and the two dogs sniffed and nudged each other. It was obvious they were happy to see one another.

"I heard from one of the ladies there that a whole heap of dogs had recently been brought into the local animal rescue. A breeder hadn't been caring for them properly. I called in to see if I could help out... and when I saw this little guy's mom, I just knew I had to take a pup when they arrived. She had a litter of three, one didn't survive, and Frank here was just such a sweetie."

We'd briefly talked about getting another Doberman one day, but I think Lawson had expected to get an adult dog, like he had with Zefer.

Frank began chewing the rug on the living room floor and Lawson frowned. "He's gonna chew everything and piss everywhere, isn't he?"

I laughed as he pulled me into his arms. "It's just stuff, cowboy. I'll buy you a new rug."

He kissed my forehead and ducked his head down to look into my eyes. "Thank you, baby – for the dog." His lips met mine.

"You're welcome," I breathed and leaned into his body. We turned and watched Zef walking around the living room, Frank right behind him. It was freaking adorable. "You're never allowed to take those two out alone, okay?"

Lawson looked at me quizzically. "What? Why not?"

"You were unbearably hot with just a dog... but a puppy? Jesus," I complained.

Lawson shrugged at me innocently. "You bought the puppy, baby."

"I clearly didn't think this through," I muttered under my breath.

He smirked and kissed me again. "Don't worry, pretty girl, you're the only one I see."

***

I spent the rest of the morning making Lawson's breakfast and baking him a birthday cake. He'd tried to tell me that he didn't need one, but I was having none of it. He was getting a damn cake.

We left it on the table to cool and headed to Logan's house to pick up all the puppy supplies. I'd gone a little mad in the store and bought a whole heap of shit we probably weren't even going to need. Lawson hadn't even told me off for it – he just shook his head and smiled while he loaded it all into the truck.

We'd had a late lunch with Logan and Q, and they were coming over for dinner tonight too. Lawson didn't know, but I'd invited some of our friends over to help celebrate his birthday.

Lawson's mom had called and sang him happy birthday. He'd told me it was a tradition that she and his nana had done every year – it was adorable.

I'd organized for Reeve and Lisa to pick up the takeout I'd ordered for tonight, so after shooing Lawson out of the kitchen, I'd iced his cake and then we'd taken Zef and Frank for their first walk together.

A couple of hours later, I looked over at my handsome fiancé as we were sitting on the back wraparound porch. It was my favorite spot, it overlooked the water and it was so beautiful to watch the sun rising and setting from there. Lawson was leaning back in his chair, relaxing. He had Frank in his lap and was stroking Zef's head, which was also in his lap. I pulled out my phone and snapped a photo of the three of them. I smiled as I looked at it on the screen.

"That's one for a frame," I told him as I spun it around so he could see.

He was wearing grey sweatpants and a black hooded sweatshirt, but he was still hotter than hell. The man could rock a sack and still look like a god. His dark hair had fallen forward onto his forehead and I was itching to lean over and run my hands through it. The more casual he looked, the more privileged I felt – it was something that hardly anyone else saw.

He was watching me, as I was watching him. I could feel his eyes prickling my skin.

"You're giving me that look, pretty girl."

My lips curved up into a smile. "I know I am."

He shook his head and chuckled deeply, his gravelly laugh sending shivers down my spine.

"It's the dogs, I swear. No one can resist a man with a puppy, let alone a man that looks like you, with a puppy."

His eyes held a challenge. "Who's saying you have to resist?"

I wiggled a finger at him. "Uh uh. Nope. You need a shower. We have plans."

He raised his eyebrows in surprise. "We do?"

I nodded in confirmation. "We do. And as sexy as you look right now, I think you should shower and change." I held out my hands for Frank, and Lawson reluctantly handed him over before kissing me on the head and going inside with a goofy smile on his face.

3. Lawson

I looked around the room and smiled. Logan and Quinn were here, Lisa and Reeve, even Rome and Josh. El had organized Thai takeout for everyone, and she'd forced me to sit still while she turned out the lights and had everyone sing me happy birthday, candles and all.

I smiled at the thought of her beautiful face as she'd watched me blow out the flames. Her eyes sparkled, and she had a huge grin on her face – it was glaringly obvious that El loved birthdays.

My phone rang loud and shrill from my pocket. I sat my beer down and pulled it out. 'Mom' flashed across the screen.

Weird... she already called.

"Hey, Mom," I answered. "What's up?"

"Lawson." Her voice was choked with tears.

I was up and out of my seat in a flash. I stalked into my office and shut the door behind me.

"What is it, Mom?"

"Oh, Lawson," she sobbed. "I'm so sorry."

"What? What's happened? You need to talk to me."

"It's your father." Her voice was no more than a whisper.

My father?

"I don't have a father." My voice was laced with venom.

"*Michael.* I'm talking about Michael."

"I'm aware of that. What the fuck has he done to you now?"

I hated the man. He had treated us like dirt; he'd left us when we needed him. He wasn't worth anything to me, and I was furious that he was still able to cause my mother pain.

"He's dead." Her sobs filled the line as I bounced the words back and forth in my head.

Dead?

I heard the door open behind me and spun around to see El pop her head in the room. She must have seen the confused expression on my face; she slid through the door and shut it softly behind her.

"He's dead," I repeated. I didn't know if I was talking to my mother or to El. I just needed to hear the words come out of my mouth.

My mother didn't respond.

"Lawson?" El asked softly. I met her big blue eyes and saw how worried she was. "Are you okay?" She walked slowly towards me.

"He's dead," I repeated again. "My father... Michael. He's dead."

I heard El's gasp and felt her hands wrap around my waist. It took me a moment to recognize it as her comforting me, for the father I'd just lost. But that wasn't the case. The man was nothing but a sperm donor – he was a stranger to me. I felt nothing.

"How?" I asked.

"Car accident. A woman was killed too... I need to tell Quinn." My mother choked out.

"I'll tell her," I told her sternly. "She's here with me now." There was no way I wanted her calling Quinn while she was in this state.

I got no response, but I could imagine her nodding into the phone.

"I have to go, Mom, I'm sorry, I'll call you tomorrow. Can you call Aunt Carol? Have her come and stay with you?" I asked her gently. I knew my mom still loved Michael Pierce. I had no fucking clue why – the man was an asshole, but the fact of the matter was that she did, and I knew she was hurting.

"She's on her way over here now."

Hearing that had me feeling a lot better about things. I didn't want my mom on her own dealing with her grief.

"Okay, good. I love you."

"I love you too."

I dropped my phone on the desk and tugged on Ellerslie's hair so that her face tilted up towards mine.

"I'm okay, baby. He hasn't been my father for a long time."

She nodded. "I know. But he's still your dad. I'm sorry, Lawson."

I pulled her back in close and rested my chin on the crown of her head. "Could you please go and get Q, baby?"

"Of course." El pulled back away from me. "Do you think she'll be okay?"

I wasn't sure how Quinn would take it. I knew she shared some of my ha-tred for the man. But just how she would feel... I didn't know. She was younger when he left, and she didn't remember a thing about him.

"I don't know, pretty girl." I sighed. "I sure hope so."

El came back a few minutes later with a confused-looking Quinn.

"What the hell is going on?" Quinn demanded with her hands on her hips.

"I'll give you two some space," El said quietly, shooting me a sympathetic glance.

"No!" I told her quickly, reaching for her hand. "Stay. You're part of our family too."

El gave me a small nod, but I saw the fire blazing in her eyes – she loved the idea of that as much as I did.

"Mom just called me. She's had some bad news." I gently led Quinn by the elbow and sat her in one of the armchairs. I sat in the other, and El perched on the arm of Quinn's chair.

"Okay..." Quinn glanced back and forth between El and I. "Is Mom okay? Fuck, she's not sick, is she?" I saw the panic in my sister's face.

"She's fine," I reassured her. I squeezed her hand. "It's Michael."

"Our dad?" Quinn asked, clearly confused by the mention of his name.

I took a deep breath and looked Quinn straight in the eyes. "He's been killed in a car accident. I don't know much more than that... just that there was a woman killed too."

Quinn opened her mouth to speak but no words came out.

I squeezed her hand and El wrapped an arm around her shoulders. "I'm sor-ry, Q."

I watched a single tear fall from Quinn's eye and roll down her cheek. It broke my heart more than the news of our father's death ever could.

"God, I'm so stupid," Quinn spat out suddenly, wiping the tear from her face. "I didn't even know him."

"It's okay to be upset, honey," El told her softly, hugging her shoulders.

"But I shouldn't be! He's never been anything to me – to *us*." Quinn looked back at me. "He's *not* our father."

I shook my head. "He gave up that right a long time ago."

Quinn let out a short, bitter laugh. "I guess I just assumed that one day he'd wake up and realize he'd fucked it all up. He'd turn back up in our lives and I'd at least get a choice." She sniveled and wiped her nose on her hand. "I would have told him to fuck off – but still, at least it would have been my choice."

I understood what Quinn was feeling. Hell, I'd been there myself. Five years ago, I'd even gone so far as to dig into his whereabouts. I found out what he did for a job, where he lived, if he was married...

At the time, he lived a couple of hours away from where we grew up; he was single and was in charge of a large company. He was doing well for himself. He'd never had any more children.

I hadn't told Quinn about any of it – I'd been embarrassed by my curiosity towards the man who'd abandoned us and left my mom heartbroken. I'd seen enough. The only thing that had stuck with me was the photo I'd seen of him; it was like looking into a mirror. I had his eyes, his skin tone, his hair... I was the spitting image of Michael Pierce.

"It's his loss," I told Quinn. "He's missed out on seeing how amazing you are. He's not worth knowing, you didn't miss out on a single thing."

"What happens now?" she asked quietly.

"I have absolutely no idea. I'll call Mom tomorrow and see if she knows anything more."

"I'm going to go and tell everyone that we'll call it a night. Do you want to stay the night, Q?" El stood as she spoke.

Quinn nodded. "I'd like that."

El gave me a small smile and left the room.

"Will you want to go to the funeral?" I asked Quinn after El shut the door.

"I have no idea. I don't even know where he lives."

"Still where he's always been I presume."

She looked at me in question.

I sighed. "I tracked him down a few years back. I don't even know why I did it." I scrubbed my hands over my face.

"What else do you know?"

"He was single, no other children, big CEO, flash house..." I told her. "I look like him," I added quietly.

She nodded. "Mom told me that. She said you were the exact image of him. She said that our eyes are from him."

I nodded. Looking at the picture of my father had been like looking at a future version of myself.

***

I watched as El opened her eyes, blinked a couple of times and snuggled back into her pillow. I chuckled as I felt her fingers reaching out, blindly feeling around for mine.

I rolled over and clasped her hand in both of mine. "Good morning, pretty girl."

She yawned loudly and opened her eyes again. "Good morning." Her eyes assessed me and narrowed. "You didn't sleep," she accused.

I shook my head. "Not really. I was thinking about Quinn and Mom. Then I started to worry about Frank downstairs in his crate, so I had to go and check on him."

"You *need* to sleep," she scolded me – the softness in her eyes telling me she wasn't really mad, just worried.

I knew she was right; the next few days would be hard on my mom. I needed to be strong to support her.

"I'll take a nap later, after I find out if Mom knows anything more."

"How did she know in the first place?"

I shrugged. I had no idea and I hadn't even thought to ask her.

I had a lot of questions, and I needed some answers.

***

"Hey, Mom. How are you?"

"I'm okay, honey. How are you and your sister holding up?"

"I'm doing alright," I told her. "Quinn stayed last night. She's having some breakfast with Ells... she's doing okay." I couldn't help the warmth that seeped into my voice at the mention of my fiancée's name.

"Good. That's good."

"Mom... how did you hear about the accident?"

"Michael's attorney called me. Apparently in the event of his death, I was to be contacted and informed, and I was to be the one to inform you both... I took to Google after that, that's how I knew that a woman had been killed too. It was all very vague – no names."

"Why?" I asked bluntly. He'd never made contact before. I couldn't understand why we would need to know that he was dead.

"I don't know. But the attorney did say he would be in touch with you as soon as he had everything put into place."

"With me? What the fuck for?"

"Lawson Pierce," my mother snapped. "Don't you use that language with me. I have no idea what your father has done or why. This is not *my* doing."

I sighed. It didn't matter how old I was, nothing made me feel like a child quite like a good telling off from Whitney Adams.

"I'm sorry, Mom. I just hate not knowing."

"I know." She let out a breath. "I'll call you if I find out more and I expect the same from you."

"Of course. Take care okay, Mom?"

"I will. Give that baby girl of mine a kiss for me."

"Sure thing. I'll talk to you soon."

I hung up and ran a hand through my hair. None of this shit made any sense. I was intrigued by the attorney's intention to contact me. The only thing I could think of was that Michael had left Quinn and I something in his will.

I abandoned my thoughts, no doubt I'd find out soon enough.

I followed the sound of the girls talking in the kitchen. I stopped and gave Q a kiss on the head. "From Mom," I prompted.

"I should call her," Quinn commented nonchalantly.

El nodded with enthusiasm. "Go call her, honey. Talking to your mom might help you to feel better about things."

Quinn slid off the stool, dialing our mother as she walked out of the room.

"What did your mom say?" El asked as she pressed herself against me.

I tugged her in even closer and kissed her forehead. "She was contacted by Michael's attorney, and asked to inform me and Quinn. I don't understand any of it... apparently this guy plans to call me."

El looked up at me and frowned. "That's weird."

"It's fucking weird alright." We stood still, holding one another for a few minutes.

"Coffee?" El asked me in a hopeful voice. I knew she was trying to distract me.

"Sounds good, baby."

She poured me a cup and I'd just lifted it to my mouth when my phone rang. The phone number was blocked.

"Lawson Pierce."

"Good morning, Mr. Pierce, this is Samuel Terry speaking."

"Good morning, Mr. Terry, how can I help you?"

"I'm calling as your father, Michael Pierce's attorney. Please accept my condolences on his passing."

"Thank you," I muttered. "Can I ask why you're calling me?"

"I think that would be better discussed in person, if you don't object."

What the fuck is going on here?

"I'm assuming Michael didn't live locally? Unfortunately, that's not exactly convenient for my sister and me."

"I'm aware of your location, Mr. Pierce, I've actually just stepped off a flight – I'm here."

"You're here?" I asked, shock and disbelief coloring my voice.

"Indeed I am. I was given a very specific set of instructions by your father."

"Okay?" I wasn't sure what the hell to do now. "Where can we meet you?"

"I'd prefer if I could come to your home. It really is a matter that needs to be discussed in private. Is that suitable?"

Jesus.

"Ah... yeah... sure?" My reply came out as a question.

"I'm very sorry for the intrusion Mr. Pierce, I have your address down as 145 Summerset Road, is that correct?"

How the fuck does he know that?

"That's correct."

"And can I assume that Miss Pierce and Miss Rush will both be present for this meeting?"

"How do you know about Ellerslie?" I spat, suddenly worried for the safety of my girl.

El shot me a 'what the fuck' look, and I shrugged.

"I apologize, I can assure you that I'll explain everything in person, is an hour's time okay?"

"Fine," I snapped. I was nearly shaking with anger. The sooner I found out what the hell was going on, and straightened this all out, the better.

I hung up and looked at El, I ran my hand through my hair in frustration. "I have no fucking idea what just happened. He knew our address; he knew about you...he's coming here in an hour."

"Well..." El huffed. "I guess we wait and see."

4. Ellerslie

Samuel Terry was a short, bald man, who wore thick-rimmed glasses. He looked around 60 years old and spoke with precision and knowledge.

Lawson had introduced Quinn and I, although I was confident Samuel needed no introductions – he knew exactly who he was dealing with, it unnerved me just how much he seemed to know about us all.

I passed him a glass of water and sat down next to Lawson on the couch. Samuel occupied one armchair and Quinn was in another.

"Once again, I offer my sincerest condolences on the passing of your father." He looked between Quinn and Lawson.

They both nodded in response.

"Can you tell us about what happened to him?" Quinn asked as she crossed her legs.

"I can." Samuel nodded. "Michael was in a car accident yesterday morning. The vehicle was struck by a truck, and he and his wife, Cassandra, were both killed instantly." His face was solemn.

"Hold on, back up a minute... his wife?" Lawson frowned.

"Yes, his wife. Michael Pierce married Cassandra Rose two years ago."

"Huh..." Quinn thought aloud.

"How old was she?" I asked when neither Quinn nor Lawson spoke again.

"She was only thirty years old." Samuel shook his head, his grief obvious.

"That's younger than me!" Lawson hissed.

I grabbed his hand in mine and squeezed. I could feel how angry he was becoming.

"I still don't understand why you're here, Mr. Terry?" Quinn asked, narrowing her eyes at the small man in front of us.

"Yes... well. I'm afraid there is more."

We all stared in silence, waiting for him to go on.

"Michael and Cassandra had a child, a daughter named Stella."

Samuel's words hung in the air. I gaped at Lawson. His jaw had dropped, and he stared directly back at me, lost for words.

The crash...

"Oh god," I whimpered. "She wasn't—"

"No," Samuel interrupted me. "She wasn't involved in the accident. She was with a sitter at the time of the crash.

I let out a relieved breath I hadn't realized I was holding.

Lawson and Q have a sister...

"What will happen to her? Does she have family to go to?" Quinn asked hurriedly.

Samuel nodded, sweat beading on his forehead. "She does."

Quinn's body sagged in relief.

"That's actually why I'm here. Michael and Cassandra had very specific instructions should anything happen to the both of them."

I felt Lawson tense next to me. "When you say that's why you're here..."

He nodded. "Mr. and Mrs. Pierce requested that their daughter, Stella Pierce, be placed in the care of you, Lawson – you and Ellerslie. They wanted for you to adopt her."

The whole world froze around me.

Me and Lawson... a kid? What the hell?

"What? No. Fuck... *what*?" Lawson stammered. "Surely Cassandra had some family?"

Samuel shook his head. "She did not. Her parents were quite old when she was born, and they have both since passed away. She was an only child. Your father's mother has also passed away, and his father has Alzheimer's. He was also an only child." He gestured to Lawson and Quinn. "The two of you are her only other living relatives."

"I'm confused," I blurted out.

"What are you unsure about, Miss Rush?"

"Call me El," I told him instinctively. "You said they appointed Lawson and me as her guardians. How did they know anything about me?" *Why would they trust a stranger with their child?"*

"Michael has kept a very close eye on both Lawson and Quinn. He was made aware of the fact that Lawson had proposed marriage to you, Ellerslie, and he only very recently adjusted his will accordingly." He picked up a folder from the coffee table. "And like I said, they didn't have any other family to consider."

The room fell silent as we all digested his words.

A child?

Well fuck me dead.

I didn't know how on earth this would work, what changes we would have to make. But we'd do it... we had to.

"How old is she?" Quinn asked quietly.

"She's five months old. She was born on the 10th of May," Samuel replied just as quietly.

She's just a baby.

My whole body shook. She would never remember her parents; she would never know their love for her.

"What if I can't take her?" Lawson asked suddenly. "I mean, what happens if I can't do it?"

"Lawson," I whispered. "She's your family." I hadn't even considered the possibility of Lawson saying no.

He angled his body towards mine. "I can't ask you to do this, El. It's too much... we're just starting out and this... it's too much."

He turned back to Samuel. "What would happen to her?"

"I'm not sure. I guess she would have to be sent to foster care until something else could be arranged. Quinn would be an option." He nodded towards my stunned-looking best friend.

I almost laughed – *almost*. Quinn wasn't the most maternal person in the world. I tugged on Lawson's arm. "Can we talk?"

He nodded and faced Samuel. "Would you excuse us please?"

"By all means," Samuel agreed.

He gripped my elbow gently and led me out of the living area and into his office. The door wasn't even shut before he started pacing.

"Sweet baby Jesus," he muttered. "What the fuck am I meant to do with this Ells? Huh? What the fuck is going on here? I thought the bastard must have left me a painting or something... not his baby... Jesus Christ."

I sat down in a seat and prepared myself to wait him out. He would pace back and forth, cursing and swearing until he calmed down.

It took him 10 minutes.

He sank down in the seat next to me. "What the fuck do I do, pretty girl?" His voice was broken. This decision was tearing him up.

"I'll tell you what's going to happen, cowboy." I grasped his hand and entwined our fingers. "We're going to go back out there, and we're going to tell him that we'll do it. We'll take that little girl."

Lawson looked like he wanted to argue so I pressed a finger to his lips.

"We're all she's got in this world, Lawson. We can't send her into foster care. We can give her everything she needs. You've got so much love, Lawson, she needs some of it."

5. Lawson

"We're all she's got in this world, Lawson…"

El's words flew through my head.

She wants her.

I'd instantly assumed that El would be too shocked to say yes – that she'd want to say no. I should have known better.

"You would take her?" I asked, the words coming out in a rush.

El nodded slowly, a look of determination on her face. "I don't think there was ever a choice."

I grabbed her face in my hands and kissed her – softly at first, then passionately. I told her how much I loved her, how much she meant to me through my kiss.

I panted against her mouth, almost entirely out of breath. "Are you sure, Ells? I would never ask this of you."

Hell, I wouldn't have asked this of myself.

"You didn't," she replied simply. Her lips were swollen and sexy from our kiss, her cheeks flushed. I'd never seen anything more beautiful in my life.

We walked back into the living room hand in hand – our minds made up. We would honor the final wishes of Stella's parents and be the family that she needed us to be.

I gave Quinn a nod. She widened her eyes in surprise, tears beginning to stream down her face.

"We'll do it," I spoke directly to Samuel.

His whole body relaxed, and he smiled at us in obvious relief. "I can't tell you how glad I am to hear you say that."

He began searching through his folder, pulling out sheets of paper. He leaned over and showed one to me.

"This document outlines their wishes for their daughter." He indicated to the page. "Basically, they would like you to raise her as your own, and they request that you make their existence known to her when she is of an appropriate age to understand. Their entire estate has been left to Stella, with you, Quinn, having the controlling interest until she reaches twenty-one years of age." He glanced briefly at Quinn.

I nodded. "That's all fine."

"There's just one more thing." Samuel pointed towards the bottom of the page. "They have stated that they wish for Stella to be formally adopted by the both of you... but only once you are married."

"We're due to be married in a few months. Can it wait?"

"It's possible. It's also possible for you to request to adopt her yourself, Lawson, and have Ellerslie included later."

I frowned at the suggestion.

"It's likely we can find a loop hole and override the condition. The sooner this happens, the easier it will be for everyone." Samuel added quickly.

"Could we meet her first? Can we worry about that when we get her home?" El asked.

Samuel nodded. "As you wish. Is there any chance of the three of you getting on a plane this week?"

I opened my mouth to speak, but El got in first. "We'll leave on the next available flight," she told him.

Samuel beamed at her. "If I may say so, I think they made a fine choice with the two of you."

They couldn't have picked a better woman than El. As for me... I wasn't so sure about that decision.

"Do you have a photo of her?" I was suddenly desperate for some type of connection with this new relative of mine.

Will she look like me?

"I have a photo here of Michael and Cassandra, but not one of Stella, I'm sorry."

"Can I see it?" El asked him with her hand already outstretched.

"Certainly." He flicked through his folder. I didn't need to see the photo of my father; I only needed to pick up a mirror to see what he looked like. It was his young wife I was curious about.

Samuel passed El the photo and I gazed down over her shoulder at it. They were dressed to the nines, my father in a tux, and Cassandra in a stunning blue dress. I studied her face; her likeness to Ellerslie was uncanny. She wasn't as tall, or as curvy, but they were similar in their hair, their eyes, and the shape of their lips.

I heard El gasp. "You're just like him."

I had barely even glanced at Michael. "She reminds me of you."

Samuel cleared his throat. "It would appear that you and Michael share not only your looks, but also your taste in women."

El passed Quinn the picture.

"Well that's just too fucking weird for words."

I chuckled at my sister's bluntness. It felt good to laugh again, even Samuel cracked a smile.

El still looked shocked. "Now I know how you'll look in twenty years," she whispered.

I squeezed her thigh lightly.

"What do we need to do from here?" I asked him, getting back to business.

"Well, as Ellerslie suggested, you should all come as soon as possible. Stella is being cared for by the sitter she was with at the time of the accident. The service for Michael and Cassandra will be held on Tuesday, so you can attend that if you wish. Then there is just the matter of their belongings, and bringing Stella back here with you."

I shook my head. "I don't think we'll need to attend the service."

"Lawson," El scolded me. "Stella needs to be there. I don't blame you for not wanting to go, but we need to put her first."

I froze. She was right. Already, she was able to put this baby first.

How would I ever be able to be a good dad to her?

"You're right." I stood quickly. "Please excuse me, I just need a minute." I strode out of the room and headed up the stairs.

"I'm sorry," I heard El say. "He's panicking."

Panicking...

That was a fucking understatement.

"Maybe it's true that we don't know what we have until we lose it, but it's also true that we don't know what we're missing until we find it."
- Author unknown

6. Ellerslie

I found Lawson exactly as I'd expected to – pacing the room and running his hand through his hair.

I stood silently in the doorway and watched him. I knew he was aware of my presence – he always was.

"I'll fuck it up." He spoke without looking at me.

He was freaking out. It was fair enough. This was a hell of a lot to take in. We were about to become parents, and without the nine months to prepare for the change. This was going to turn our lives upside down.

"We'll fuck it up together," I replied softly.

He stopped pacing and snapped his head around to look at me. "That's not very reassuring, baby."

I snorted. "It's true. Neither of us has any idea of what we're getting into. But we'll get through it. We'll do our best, Lawson. It's all we can do."

He stared at me – pain in his eyes. "What if it breaks us?"

There it was; his fear of losing me was holding him back.

"I can't lose you." His voice cracked.

I walked towards him. "You won't."

"She's not even ours—"

"She's ours now," I interrupted him.

He grabbed me and tugged me against his chest. I felt him breathing in the vanilla scent of my hair, trying to calm himself down. His tense muscles started to loosen.

"We're strong. We'll be strong for her too," I told him. "The only thing that will break us is if you run. I need you to run *to* me, not away from me."

He sighed and squeezed me tighter. "No more running."

No more running.

***

I glanced out the cab window – this city was quite a sight. We'd had to wait until early Monday morning to get a flight out. It had taken a little under six hours, and I hadn't slept a wink. Lawson hadn't either. Quinn was the only one who had managed to get any rest, and even then, it was no more than a couple of hours.

We'd left the dogs with Logan, and arranged to have at least this week off work. Quinn hoped to get back into the office when we returned later in the week.

I was so nervous. The thought of seeing Stella was terrifying. I knew Lawson wasn't doing too well either. He was touching me constantly and kissing me often. I knew he needed me close to keep him sane.

It gave me butterflies in my stomach – knowing that I could be an anchor for him. He was exactly that for me. He was my rock.

"What if she hates me?" Lawson muttered quietly.

I couldn't help it, I laughed at him. "She's just a baby, Lawson, she doesn't know how to hate."

He huffed out a breath and stayed silent for the remainder of the ride.

The cab pulled up outside a tall apartment building. We'd given the driver the address that Samuel had provided. He was meeting us here and would be introducing us to both Caroline – Stella's babysitter, and to Stella herself.

My hands were shaking as I stepped out onto the pavement.

Lawson must have sensed my distress – he pulled me into his arms and held me tightly, running his hands through my long blonde hair.

"I love you so much, El."

"I love you more," I whispered back the reply that had become habit for us.

I took a deep steadying breath and tipped my head back to look up at the up-market building. This was it... there was no going back from this. As of today, we would be a family.

"You guys ready?" Quinn asked loudly, pulling me from my thoughts.

Lawson shrugged. "Ready as I'll ever be."

I gave her a small smile and took Lawson's hand in mine.

***

"It's just this door right here," Samuel told us nervously. We stood outside apartment number one hundred and twenty-five. I wondered idly if Michael and Cassandra had planned to bring their daughter up in this building. I believed children should have space – room to run around and play. That was the way I'd imagined raising my children one day, and I knew Lawson would agree with me.

Samuel knocked, and I heard the sound of feet padding across the floor. The woman who opened the door was older than I'd expected. She was short, her graying hair was pulled back into a loose bun, and she had wrinkles around her eyes.

She smiled warmly at us all. "Come in everyone, I'm Caroline."

We filed in, each of us introducing ourselves to her.

She stopped at Lawson. "My gosh, you are just the spitting image of your father, Lawson."

He looked uncomfortable. "So I've been told," He murmured quietly.

She led us into the living area. The apartment was impressive. Expensive furnishings filled the space and large paintings hung on the walls.

"Stella is due to wake any time now, can I get you a drink while we wait?"

We all politely declined.

"Where do you live, Caroline?" I asked her as I peered out the window that overlooked the city below.

"Oh, just down the hall, love. I've known Michael and Cassandra for three years." She turned around to face Lawson and Quinn. "I am terribly sorry for your loss."

Lawson tensed. "I don't mean to be rude, but to be completely honest with you, we haven't lost a thing. Michael hasn't been a part of our lives since we were very young. You knew him better than we did, so I'm sorry for *your* loss."

Caroline nodded. "Yes… he told me about the two of you; how he regretted what he'd done… he wished he could take it back, you know?"

"Too little, too late," I heard Quinn mumble.

Caroline didn't hear her. "You know what I think? I think that's why he's put this on to you now. I don't think he could have forgiven himself if he had taken another family member from you."

Lawson was getting agitated; he had been bouncing his knee up and down as he sat.

I placed a hand firmly on his leg and smiled at Caroline. "Would it be okay if you ran through Stella's routine with us?" I asked her, taking the focus away from Lawson.

"Certainly, honey." She sat down on the couch and gestured for me to join her.

I moved to the space next to her, pulled out a pen and paper and wrote down every single little thing the older woman said.

***

Samuel had left us with Caroline a half hour ago, he had an important meeting to get to, but he assured us he was available for us to contact if there was anything at all we needed.

I heard the light cries through the baby monitor at the same time Caroline did. "She's awake." She pushed up to her feet and headed off down the hallway.

My heart was beating out of my chest. I was sitting a few meters away from Lawson and my body needed to be near his. I hopped up swiftly and a nervous giggle slipped past my lips as I saw him doing the same thing. We met halfway across the space.

"Here we go," he said softly, searching my eyes for signs of panic.

I relaxed at his proximity and smiled.

"Oh my god... she's beautiful," I heard Quinn squeak.

I spun around, and my eyes locked on the precious little girl in Caroline's arms.

Her big green eyes flicked back and forth between Quinn and I before finally landing on Lawson.

She's just like him.

Stella looked so much like Lawson, but at the same time, I could see her mother in her. Her skin tone wasn't as olive as Lawson's; it was more of a golden tone, like mine. She had a small amount of light hair on her head, but the most captivating thing about her was easily her eyes. Quinn and Lawson's big green eyes were repeated exactly into her sweet little face.

Beautiful doesn't even cover it...

I squeezed Lawson's hand. "Wow," I breathed.

Stella shrieked and held a hand out toward Lawson.

Caroline walked her over towards us slowly – Stella's eyes never leaving Lawson's face.

I turned slightly to watch, riveted to the spot, and knew Quinn was too. Nobody said a word.

Caroline stopped right in front of Lawson and held Stella out. Lawson reached towards her, his hands shaking slightly. Stella shrieked again and thrust her hands out towards him, wanting to be held.

She loves him already.

I could feel the tears streaming down my face at the pure magic of this moment. It dawned on me then that we would be okay; we would be able to overcome anything that this new challenge would throw at us.

"She wants you to hold her," Caroline told Lawson gently.

"I... I don't know how," he stammered.

Caroline ignored his protests and gently passed Stella into his arms. He made an awkward-looking cradle and tucked her against his body.

My heart swelled at the sight of the two of them together. They were so perfect.

I needed to get a ring on that man's finger. He looked even hotter with a baby than he did with a puppy.

Quinn stepped quietly over to where we stood. Lawson still holding Stella, with me pressed against his side, both of us staring at the wonder in his arms.

"She's so stunning," Quinn whispered as she stroked Stella's small hand.

I nodded in agreement.

"She's a pretty little thing alright," Lawson replied quietly, a small smile on his lips.

"My turn," Quinn demanded – breaking the moment.

Lawson chuckled, but handed her over. He gently slid Stella from his arms into Quinn's. Stella struggled to keep her eyes on Lawson – even letting out a small wail, but when she finally met Quinn's gaze, she calmed down, it was as though she recognized the blood ties the three of them shared.

I wiped the sweat from my hands onto my jeans. I didn't have any connection to Stella.

Would she sense that? What if it's me she doesn't like?

"Relax, baby." Lawson leaned in and murmured in my ear. "She'll love you as much as I do."

7. Quinn

Well fucking hell. This was a lot – like, A LOT, a lot.

They were parents now... my best friend and my big brother had their own little family.

Sweet baby Jesus.

Life just went from partying to diapers real quick.

I am so glad it's not me.

I felt like a selfish bitch for thinking that, but hell, it was true. I was not at the stage in my life where I was ready for a baby. I would have taken her – in a heartbeat... but I wouldn't have been anywhere near ready. And Colt... god I couldn't even imagine what he would have done. He was just a baby himself.

A really, really persistent baby...

Lawson and El... they could handle this – they were solid.

I looked down at the sweet little girl in my arms. I loved her already. She was the most beautiful baby I'd ever seen in my life and I was going to be the coolest aunty in the world.

I glanced at El, she was nervous. I would be too; meeting a baby that would eventually call me Mom... it was fucking huge.

I can't believe she's going to be a mom!

I had to admit it was hard being here, seeing that the man whose name was written on my birth certificate had wanted this family, but hadn't wanted mine.

Hadn't wanted me...

I knew I shouldn't give a fuck, but part of me did, just a tiny bit.

Stella squirmed in my arms and snapped me out of it.

"Your turn, El," I announced, and stepped towards the only sister I'd ever known – at least until now.

"Oh okay... shit—" El clapped a hand over her mouth. "Did I just swear in front of her already?" she whispered, clearly horrified.

"Who gives a fuck?" I crooned in my best baby voice. "You don't have a clue... do you, baby girl?"

"Quinn!" El snapped playfully. "Give her here before she starts cussing like a sailor."

"Here you go, Momma," I said quietly as I passed her over.

El gaped at the name and I saw tears shining in her eyes.

"You're her mom now, El," I told her in a whisper.

She nodded and bit down on her lip, I knew she was trying to reign in her emotions and hold back the tears that were threatening to fall.

The minute El had Stella in her arms her body began to automatically rock slowly from side to side. They locked eyes and it was as though they'd known each other forever.

I let out the breath I didn't even realize I'd been holding.

They're all gonna be okay.

Lawson stepped behind El and wrapped his arms around her waist. I could hear El talking softly to Stella, but I couldn't make out the words – they were just for the three of them.

I pulled out my phone and quietly took a few photos.

I would never forget this moment, not for the rest of my life. The photos were for Stella, so she could look back on this day, and see the first moment she was loved unconditionally by her second set of parents.

"Sometimes it knocks the breath right out of me, realizing how lucky I am to be here and alive with you. To be the one you feel safe with. To be the one whose bones you curl up into when it's cold. To be the one whose mouth you drowsily kiss when you are half asleep in my arms."

- Beau Taplin

8. Lawson

How the fuck did I get so lucky?

El was a complete natural with Stella; it was as though she was born to be a mother.

We'd been here all afternoon, learning her cues, feeding and changing her. Caroline had stayed with us, and I was grateful; we were essentially still strangers to Stella and I didn't want to frighten her.

We didn't seem like strangers though…

It was clear to see that she was comfortable with both El and I. She had barely cried, she smiled often and babbled away at us constantly.

The one time she had gotten upset, El had passed her to me while she went to find a bottle – I'd looked into her eyes and she'd calmed down. It wasn't hard to figure out why. I'd never been happier to look like my father, I was just grateful that being his spitting image would help this little girl transition into our lives.

"She's asleep," El told me quietly as she tip-toed into the room and sank down onto the couch.

Caroline followed her out and laughed. "You don't need to be quiet, honey, that little girl sleeps like the dead. You won't hear from her again until morning."

"You're not staying?" I asked, suddenly nervous.

"I'm just down the hall, but you won't need me, she'll be out to it for at least the next ten hours."

"Really?" El gaped. "Aren't babies meant to wake up all the time?"

"Not this one. She's slept solidly through the night since she was ten weeks old. She's a real dream in that respect." Caroline began collecting her various items from around the room. "The first hiccup might come when we run out of breast milk; she's never tried formula before."

"I'll run out and get her some tomorrow," El said, making a note on her phone. "At least we know she'll take a bottle."

"If she's anything like her aunty, she'll drink anything," Quinn teased.

"That sounds weird." I shook my head and grinned at her. "Aunty Quinn."

"You know what sounds weirder?"

I laughed – I knew where this was going.

Q pointed at me. "You're a daddy."

I knew she expected me to look stunned, shocked… even a little horrified maybe.

"I guess I am." I chuckled. "Who the hell would have thought, huh?"

El gave me a megawatt smile and snuggled into my side. Quinn huffed – she was hoping I'd flip.

Not this time, little sis.

***

El had checked Stella about half a dozen times since Caroline left us, before conceding that she did in fact, sleep like the dead.

I'd even given in to the urge, checking myself, and sure enough, she was out to it.

"Okay, so what will happen to all of this?" El waved her hand around, gesturing to all of the belongings.

I looked at Quinn; it was her decision to make.

"Well it's all going to have to go." She glanced around. "I was thinking it might be nice for Stella if you took some of the paintings to hang at home – you know, so she has some familiar sights."

It was a good idea.

"I'll arrange to have them packaged up," I told the girls.

"Obviously we'll take everything of Stella's with us," Quinn went on. "I think the rest should just be brought back with us and stored, and the apartment rented. That way it will make Stella some money, and she can decide what she wants to do with it all when she's older."

I nodded. I was happy Quinn was on the ball with all of this; my head was all caught up in bottles, sleep times and diapers. I was betting El's was too.

How the hell we were going to run two companies, operate the restaurant, care for Stella and the dogs, and still find time for each other was beyond me. The phrase 'bitten off more than you can chew' flashed through my mind.

"Lawson?" El nudged me in the side.

"Huh?"

"Quinn asked if there is anything here you want to take?"

"Oh right. Sorry. I don't think so, but I'll take a look."

Quinn started making notes on her phone, probably of all the things she'd need to have moved.

"Are you okay?" El whispered.

I smiled as I brushed a strand of hair from her face. "I'm fine; I guess I'm just worried about how we'll manage our lives when we get back."

El sighed. "I wondered the same thing. We both work so much."

"I think I'll cut down on my hours," I told her. "Logan is too good to be a project manager; I could promote him to my second in charge. He can handle it."

"But you love your work," El protested.

I chuckled softly. "So, you're telling me that you haven't already thought about how you can spend less time in the office?"

El blushed and gave me a guilty smile.

I thought so.

I tapped the end of her nose. "You love your work too, baby."

"I think I already love her more," she whispered, snuggling in even closer to me.

Yup... I'm the luckiest son of a bitch in the world...

***

Caroline was right – we didn't hear a peep from Stella until half past seven in the morning. Even then it was just a quiet jabbering that I could hear through the baby monitor.

"I'll get her." I yawned, getting no response from El. I rolled over, but she was already gone.

"Good morning, precious girl," El's sweet voice came through the monitor. "You slept for such a long time." I heard the sounds of her diaper being changed and then the sucking noises of El feeding her a bottle. It made me smile.

I think I could get used to this.

"You have a big day today, little girl. We have to say goodbye to your mommy and daddy," I heard El's voice crack a little at the statement.

I jumped out of the bed and threw on some pants. My heart melted at what I heard next.

"But it's okay, you have us now and we'll do everything in this world to care for you... you will have so much love in your life, Stella."

I quietly made my way to Stella's door. They were sitting together in the rocking chair, Stella propped up in El's arms.

Seeing the two of them together like that ... everything fell into place. A wave of sadness washed over me for the parents she'd lost – ones that she'd never remember. It was quickly chased away by a burst of gratitude, to my father. He may have been an absolute prick, but he hadn't denied me or Stella this, he had given us the chance to be a family.

Ellerslie and I would make sure Stella's life was never anything but full.

9. Ellerslie

The past few days had been some of the most draining I'd ever experienced. Lawson, Quinn and I had taken Stella to farewell her parents. It was an incredibly emotional experience. There were so many people there to meet, talk to, and receive condolences from.

I'd thought Lawson was going to lose it if he had to hear one more 'I'm sorry for your loss'.

I was glad he was there for their service, in time he would be glad too.

I think he'd finally put his anger towards his father to rest. He had more important things to focus on now.

We'd gone through every belonging in the apartment yesterday, taking the things we thought would be useful for Stella, and packing up the rest for storage. Lawson had arranged for a company to come and package the paintings. They were being shipped to our house along with all the furniture and items from Stella's nursery.

I lightly bounced Stella up and down on my knee as she stared out the window of the plane. We were about to descend and take her home for the first time.

She was the sweetest baby, only crying if she was hungry or needing a diaper change, and they were easy fixes. If she was tired, she slept – wherever she was. It was as though she knew this was a lot for us to take on, and she was making it as easy as possible.

I'd spoken with Reeve about the adoption several times. We needed to start the process as soon as possible, the only trouble being that we weren't married yet. That meant that Lawson might have to do it alone. He'd said he wasn't adopting her without me – so we were at an impasse. The last thing we needed was a problem occurring in the next few months while we waited for the wedding – it was unlikely, but it was a risk I didn't like taking. Reeve was busy searching for a loop hole on the marriage condition.

"The apartment is already rented," Quinn told me as she leaned around Lawson's sleeping body.

"Wow that was quick. How much is it going for?"

Quinn held out her phone to show me the figure.

"Holy shit!" I replied a little too loudly. I shot the older gentleman down the row an apologetic glance. "Go Stella."

She was going to make a fortune off that place. Michael and Cassandra had owned it outright, and now it was hers.

"It was a good call keeping it, Q." I shot Quinn a grateful look. I had so much on my plate with baby stuff; I was so glad that we could rely on her. She would always look out for Stella's best interests.

Quinn reached around and held her hand out to Stella – she wrapped her tiny hand around Q's finger.

"Are you doing okay with all this, El? I wouldn't blame you if you were freaking out."

I *was* freaking out – completely freaking out. But at the same time, I was at peace with it all. She was a part of my life now, a big part of my life. Already I knew I wouldn't give her up for anything.

"I am worried about how we'll find time for everything," I confessed, fiddling with Stella's tights. I glanced at Lawson to make sure he was still sleeping. "I'm worried we'll lose some of the magic we've got... we won't have the same time for each other as we do now."

Quinn nodded.

"Don't get me wrong... I want her, I really do. She's ours now... but I just found him, you know?"

"I get it, girl." Quinn looked at me in understanding. "But I don't think you have anything to worry about... Lawson is so in love with you, El. He won't let anything tear the two of you apart. If anything, he'll find a way to make her bring you closer together."

I smiled. She was probably right. Lawson had a way of finding the positive in a shitty situation.

"I really hope you're right."

***

"This is it, baby girl." I walked Stella slowly down the hallway as Lawson put down our suitcases.

"This is your new home, Stella," I heard Lawson's deep voice from behind us.

Stella cooed at the sound of his voice. She loved him.

I don't blame her.

"Should we get her settled in for the night?" Lawson asked.

"Do you want a bath, Stella girl? Huh? A nice warm bath?" I crooned to her and kissed her cheeks.

She giggled and squirmed in my arms.

"Let's go, my beautiful girls."

Swoon.

***

It was official. Stella was an absolute trooper. We'd given her a nice long bath, filled her to the brim with milk, and put her down in the room closest to ours, in a portable cot we'd purchased on our way home from the airport.

She hadn't batted an eyelid.

I was waiting for it... waiting for the shit to hit the fan. She'd gotten a little upset and vomited a bit when we'd had to switch from the breast milk to baby formula, but so far that was the biggest problem we'd had.

It was too good to be true.

Life had taught me, if something was too good to be true – then it probably was.

Only one exception sprang to mind...

Lawson.

He was far too good to be true, but he was mine.

My phone pinged with a message.

"Hey, honey, I'm sorry, but I can't get around this marriage clause. I'll call you tomorrow about the options we have."

"Reeve text," I called out to Lawson. "He can't find a way out of this marriage thing. I'll talk to him tomorrow."

"Shit." Lawson walked out of the bathroom, flicking the light off behind him. "I was counting on him sorting that crap out. My fucking father had to do something to make life difficult, didn't he? Giving us his daughter wasn't quite enough." He huffed out a breath in frustration, running his hand through his hair.

I was suddenly so tired. I held my arms out for Lawson and he hopped into the bed, snuggling in next to me.

I held him close and ran my fingers softly down his arms.

"We'll sort it out tomorrow, cowboy. Get some sleep."

***

Why the fuck didn't I think of that before?

I sat up straight in bed. We'd been back home for two days; all of Stella's things had arrived last night and were still cluttering up the hallway.

Lawson moaned and rolled back over, he was still asleep.

I couldn't believe my mind hadn't made this connection before now.

I wonder if I can use baby brain as an excuse?

I slipped out of bed and grabbed my robe as I made my way out the door. I popped my head in to check on Stella – she was still out to it as well.

My mind was going crazy with ideas and possibilities.

I pulled up Quinn's number on my phone and hit the call button as I walked down the stairs.

"Hello?" Quinn's voice was groggy and disoriented.

Oops...

"Hell, what time is it?"

"It is..." she paused to look at the screen of her phone. "Six in the morning, El. What the fuck?"

I held back a giggle. "Sorry, but it's important."

She yawned, and I heard her getting comfortable. "Go on..."

"So, you know how Reeve can't find a way to get around the marriage condition for the adoption—"

"Yeah... it sucks," Quinn interrupted with a yawn.

"Yeah." I curled my legs underneath me as I sat down on the couch. "But I had an idea of how to fix it..."

"Wait until after the wedding, right?" Quinn prompted. "Isn't that what you decided?"

"No." I shook my head. "Well yes, but no."

Quinn yawned again. "Get on with it, Rush. It's too early for this shit."

"We'll just get married now."

"Right now?" Quinn's voice went up a couple of octaves.

"Right now... as in today." I nodded enthusiastically even though she couldn't see me.

Quinn laughed.

"What?" I demanded.

"I'm assuming you haven't told Lawson this plan yet?"

"He's still asleep."

"I'll tell you what, you call me back and let me know what he has to say."

"You don't think he'll go for it? He's become a lot more spontaneous lately, right?"

Quinn laughed again. "Yeah... just maybe not quite to this extreme."

"Put twenty bucks on it?" I taunted her.

"Make it fifty." I could practically see her smug grin from here.

"Better pick out an outfit to wear to my wedding, girl."

"Well since you're so cocky, what exactly are you planning to wear?"

Shit...

"Bitch," I muttered.

"Call me back and let me know when I'll see my money." Quinn was laughing again.

I hung up. I had more important things to do.

Convince Lawson...

Find a dress...

Fuck.

10. Lawson

I woke up and just about jumped out of my skin.

"Fuck... you scared me."

El was perched on my side of the bed, wide awake and staring at me. It wasn't the way the day usually started; I was always the one waking her up.

"Sorry, cowboy." Her eyes were sparkling, and her cheeks were flushed.

"What's going on?" I questioned warily.

"I have a plan." She grinned.

I propped myself up on my elbow so I could see her better. "Okay... let's hear it then."

"Marry me."

I chuckled. "That's my line, baby."

She grinned even bigger. "You take my line then."

I had no idea where this was going, but I played along anyway. "Okay, it goes something like... I already agreed to that, right?"

Her eyes gleamed with victory. "Marry me *today*," she stated, stealing the last line from me too.

I chuckled at her again.

"Marry me today, Lawson," she said again more softly.

I stopped laughing as I took in the seriousness of her expression.

She's not joking.

"But the wedding?"

"I don't need the wedding."

"The plans?" I insisted.

"Fuck the plans," she replied.

"El." I took her hands in mine. "Slow down. Why do you want to get married today?"

She sighed and wriggled into the space next to me, staring at the ceiling. "For Stella... for me... for you... for *us*. Because I want to marry you and make our family official." She rolled over onto her side and looked into my eyes.

"But what about all the planning you've done?" I protested.

She smiled softly. "Every plan we had went out the door the minute she came along."

I thought about what she was saying. I knew she was right. Stella had changed our whole future.

"You'd do that for her?"

"It's the least I'd do for her, and for our family."

Holy shit.

My pulse sped up at the realization that she could be my wife by the end of the day. I rolled myself on top of her, supporting my weight with my arms. "Are you sure, baby? We can find another way to adopt her."

She smiled up at me. "I've never been surer about anything in my entire life."

She's going to be my wife.

Fucking finally...

***

El was running around like a headless chicken. She'd already called Quinn and I'd overheard her gloating about what she was going to buy with her fifty bucks.

Those two are mad together.

I was feeding Stella baby porridge in the kitchen while El was on the phone talking to Reeve.

"I don't care, Reeve, it's happening today. We'll have a party or whatever another day and celebrate with everyone then," El told him forcefully.

I grinned at Stella as she watched El flying around the room. "She's arguing with your uncle, baby girl. Mommy's turned into bridezilla."

El flicked me with a tea towel and pointed a warning finger at me.

Stella shrieked and giggled, spitting her breakfast everywhere in the process.

"See what I mean, Stella?" I stage whispered to the beautiful, smiling little girl in front of me.

"I am getting married today, Reeve, whether you come or not. So maybe you should reschedule that appointment."

I waited with a smirk on my face. There was no way that Reeve was going to miss this, and El knew it.

"That sounds like a great idea. See you in a couple of hours." She dropped the phone on the counter.

I glanced over and caught the triumphant smile on her face – we were all such suckers for that woman.

"He'll be here?" I asked with a chuckle.

"Of course he'll be here." El rolled her eyes at me as though I was crazy for ever doubting her ability to persuade her big brother. "Now you, Miss Stella... what are we going to put you in for this special day? Huh, baby girl?" El crooned as she wiped the mess off Stella's chin.

"I think you've got bigger things to worry about, pretty girl. What are *you* going to wear?"

She scrunched up her nose and breathed out a sigh. "I have no idea. I'll find something perfect in the wardrobe."

I held back a shudder. The last time El had attempted to 'find something perfect in the wardrobe', it was a disaster. Suddenly nothing fit right or matched her shoes or blah, blah, blah. She was, of course, dead wrong – everything she put on looked amazing, but there was no convincing her of that.

We did not have time for that kind of a meltdown today.

"Could you finish up with Stella? I just want to check if my shirt needs ironing."

"Sure, cowboy."

El took the spoon from me and I took off up the stairs – I had some important calls to make.

I dialed the number as I shut the bedroom door.

"Well, well, well. I was wondering how long it'd take for you to call me with a problem," Quinn answered with a laugh.

"Yeah, yeah," I replied gruffly. "It's not me that has the problem anyway."

"I'm listening," Q replied.

"El doesn't have a dress. Any chance you could save the day in that department again?"

"I'm way ahead of you," Quinn answered smugly. "I've been searching online for the past hour and I've called the store and had them put the perfect dress on hold for me. I'll pick it up when the store opens at ten."

Oh, thank fuck for that.

"You're a lifesaver, Q. Will it fit? It won't need altering or whatever?"

"Would you just trust me?" She snapped in a pissy tone.

I chuckled. "Sorry. I trust you. Thank you, Quinn."

"I should damn well think so," she teased.

"What color is her dress? I'll need to try and match a tie."

"God, you underestimate me, big brother. I've got this. Just worry about what you're going to say when you get up there."

I smirked. That was one thing I was not concerned about. I knew exactly how I felt about El; the words were going to be easy.

11. Ellerslie

Having a lawyer for a brother certainly had its perks. Reeve had sorted everything for the changes we needed for our marriage license.

I'm going to be his wife today.

Lawson had rushed off upstairs looking like he was freaking out. When he'd come back down he was far more relaxed.

Thank fuck.

I couldn't deal with this if he wasn't one hundred percent in with me.

I'd attempted to go upstairs and find something to wear about five times now. I knew I was wasting my time – the perfect dress was not in there... I had to wear something though, but Lawson kept trying to distract me. He'd needed help finding his shoes, Stella needed more food all of a sudden, and the excuses went on and on.

"For fuck's sake, Lawson, I need to go and pick a dress." I was beyond frustrated at this point.

Lawson opened his mouth to speak but was interrupted by a knock at the door.

Just great. Who the hell is visiting now...

I stomped off in the direction of the door and threw it open with a little more force than was necessary.

"Quinn?"

She had two garment bags slung over her arm and a giant bag that was stuffed full in her other hand.

"That's right, bitch, I'm here to save the day." She barged through the door, pushing me aside as she went.

"What the hell have you got in there?" I swung the door shut and trailed behind her into the living area.

Quinn looked at me like I was stupid. "Your dress."

My mouth fell open, and I spun to narrow my eyes at Lawson. "You knew?" I couldn't help the silly grin that spread across my face.

Quinn dumped the bags down on the couch and Lawson passed Stella to her before wrapping his arms around my waist.

"I told you that you wouldn't find the perfect dress in that wardrobe." His husky voice tickled at my senses.

"Thank you, cowboy."

"Hmm hmm," Quinn cleared her throat loudly.

"Thank you, Q." I laughed without taking my eyes from my handsome husband-to-be.

"Don't worry, Stella girl, I got you something pretty too." Quinn started unzipping the bags.

"Ah, get out!" I shoved Lawson away in the direction of the door. "You can't see anything."

His look of shock was quickly replaced with one of amusement. "Okay, okay, I get it." He strolled in the direction of the kitchen. "It's such a traditional day and all..." he teased over his shoulder.

I waved him away with a flick of my wrist and a grin. I didn't have time for his jokes.

"Please tell me you have shoes?" I begged Quinn.

"I have shoes."

"Oh, thank god. What the hell would I do without you?"

"You'd rummage through your wardrobe, spit the dummy and piss off your fiancé?" she offered.

I rolled my eyes.

Smart bitch.

Quinn opened the giant bag and pulled out the cutest little silver dress I'd ever seen.

"Oh hell, that is amazing!" I squealed as I grabbed for the tiny dress.

"I know, right?"

Quinn rummaged through the bag again and pulled out some white tights and little silver Mary Jane's.

"Look, Stella, you are gonna be so pretty."

Stella shrieked at the mention of her name and tossed her toy giraffe across the room.

Stella was going to steal the show in this dress. There was no way I was putting her in it yet, she'd probably puke all over it within five minutes.

"Okay, are you ready?" Quinn asked as she unzipped one of the garment bags.

I nodded as I set down Stella's outfit and turned my full attention to the dress I would get married in.

Quinn took a deep breath and pulled out the most stunning dress I'd ever seen. The underlay was white, with a stunning silvery grey lace and tulle overlay. It was full length and sleeveless and I absolutely adored it.

"Holy shit, Q," I whispered.

"Holy shit, good?" she asked nervously.

"Holy shit, *amazing*." I nodded. I reached out to touch the fabric. It was gorgeous. I couldn't have chosen a dress more perfect if I'd tried.

"Well, thank god for that."

I laughed at Quinn's relief. "Thank you so much, it's perfect."

"You're going to look so beautiful, El."

I could feel tears building in my eyes and I quickly blinked them back. "Show me what you got for yourself."

Quinn had chosen a full length, long-sleeved navy-blue dress that would look absolutely flawless on her, whilst still being simple and understated. I had a feeling she had intentionally chosen something so simple to highlight my dress.

"It's beautiful, Q." A tear escaped my control.

"Hey? What is it?" she asked, concern on her face.

"Nothing," I spluttered, more tears spilling over. "I'm just happy. He makes me so happy. I didn't think I'd ever have this much love in my life." I glanced down at Stella as I spoke.

I truly have everything.

Quinn pulled me in and squeezed me tight. "You deserve it, babe. I'm insanely jealous, but I'm so thrilled for you, El. The two of you are going to be so happy together."

"The three of us," I amended. I pulled apart from her and swiped the tears away.

Quinn bent down, scooped up Stella and lifted her into the air. "Yeah... the three of you," she crooned through giggles. "Alright, Stella girl. Let's make Mommy gorgeous."

12. Quinn

It fit her like a second skin. I'd never, ever seen anyone look so stunning.

I knew it was a wedding dress, not exactly the kind of thing a person tended to wear more than once, but screw it – I'd make sure she wore this again if it killed me.

"You are one hundred percent having a party to celebrate this marriage," I told El as I pulled the zipper gently into place up her back.

"Huh?" she asked, confusion in her voice.

"Everybody needs to see you in this dress."

She giggled and shrugged.

"No, I'm serious, El. You look beautiful. Every single person you know needs to see this perfection. Hell, maybe you could even invite that little fucker Baxter and his bitch too."

El snorted and laughed. "You're out of your god damn mind if you think I'd invite the two of them within one hundred miles of me – no matter how good I look."

I'd done her makeup only minimal; I'd decided there was no sense in covering up her smooth golden skin with heavy foundation. I'd made her eyes stand out and let her natural beauty do the rest. Her hair was tamed into loose waves and pinned back loosely off her face, with the length trailing down her back. It was about all we had time for.

"How's he doing?" El asked nervously.

I didn't need to ask who she was talking about.

"He's doing fine."

He's freaking the hell out.

"He's losing his shit, isn't he?" she replied calmly.

She knew the man well.

"Little bit." I flicked her hair one last time and looked over her shoulder at her in the full-length mirror. "He'll be fine."

"I should go see him." El moved to take a step forward.

"Ah, ah, ah." I pulled her gently back by the arm. "He's fine. Logan and Reeve have him under control. He's got Stella with him. He's fine."

"Stop saying fine." El grinned and swatted at my hand.

"Fine," I teased.

"Did you get him his tie?" she asked, an almost panicked look on her face.

I rolled my eyes behind her back. They were as bad as each other. Absolutely zero faith in me. "Yes. I gave him his tie."

Wish everyone would just calm the hell down.

El pinched me on the hip. "I can hear that tone in your voice..." She had a huge grin on her face.

I laughed. "Well just relax. You both are as tightly wound as each other. It's all taken care of, okay? Just trust me."

She turned around and pulled me into her and squeezed me tight. "I love you, Q. Thank you."

"I love you too," I replied.

I left El fussing over herself in the mirror and slipped on my own dress. It was a beautiful dress. On any other day it would have been an eye catcher, but not today, not with El in the room.

I'd never seen my best friend so happy. So happy and so nervous at the same time. She was nothing like this on the day she married Baxter, she was completely blasé about the entire thing; she wasn't worried about a single detail. I didn't think I could recall her asking about Baxter even once on the morning of their wedding.

I guess things were different now... he was the one. I thought about all of the firsts that Lawson and Ellerslie would have together, and I could almost understand why they were freaking out. Everything was so important, so monumental when you were sharing it with the person you were meant to be with.

My thoughts drifted back to Colt and how wrong it felt between the two of us, I'd been trying to end it, I really had. But he was sweet and kind, and so close to being right for me... but just... not. It just *wasn't* right. He had feelings for me, I knew he did, and I knew it was wrong to keep seeing him when I didn't feel the same way. He just wouldn't let me end it. I shook it off; it was a problem I would have to deal with another day.

I knocked on the door to the games room before going inside.

"How's it going in here, boys?" I asked before I got a proper look at them.

Shit they looked good.

"Wow," I whispered.

All three of them flashed me megawatt smiles. "We scrub up alright, huh?" Logan chuckled.

I nodded slowly. "You look amazing."

They all had a tux on. Lawson had the silver bow tie I'd got for him paired with a black tux and a simple white on white striped shirt. He looked so handsome.

I caught sight of Stella in her dress, Reeve holding her. "Oh hell, Stella girl, this is meant to be Mommy's big day."

"She's a stunner, isn't she?" Reeve smiled fondly at his new niece as he jiggled her up and down gently.

"Such a beauty," I agreed as I took her hand and kissed it softly.

"Is El ready?" Lawson asked me. I could hear the excitement vibrating through his voice.

"She's ready." I tapped Stella's nose lightly and turned to look at my brother. "And she's perfect." I smiled at him.

"I know she is." You could see the love and adoration he had for her pouring out of him. This was the happiest I'd ever seen him.

I couldn't help it, I pulled him in for a tight hug. "I'm so proud of you," I murmured into his shoulder. "You are such a good man, Lawson."

"I'm nervous," he admitted quietly.

I released him and laughed. "You don't say?" I squeezed his shoulder. "C'mon, it's time to go."

Logan clapped him on the back, Lawson took a deep, calming breath, and they walked out the door.

"She scares the hell out of me and calms my soul at the same time. Maybe that's what love is – a total contradiction that somehow balances."
- Tammara Webber

13. Lawson

This was it. I glanced at my watch for what felt like the hundredth time.

Quinn had sent Logan and me to the courthouse early. She'd organized a limousine to pick us up from the house and there was another one waiting behind it that would take Quinn, Stella, Reeve and El.

We weren't having a traditional wedding day, but Q had insisted that El would be walking down a makeshift aisle. Reeve would give her away to me.

I had to admit, the thought of her walking towards me looking so absolutely stunning, because I already knew she'd be breathtaking, was what had me fidgeting and twitching in my seat.

Logan sat next to me and nudged me every few minutes when I started to get too jumpy. I'd shot him about fifty apologetic glances.

I looked down the long corridor again. The doors we had entered through had opened exactly twelve times since I'd sat in this seat. Each time my eyes flashed down there, I searched for her, and each time I'd come up empty. I looked down at my hands and tried to sit still.

C'mon, El.

I needed to touch her, see her... smell her. She calmed me down in a way no one else ever had or ever could.

"You ready, man?"

Was I ready?

I looked back at my best mate, my best man today. "Fuck yeah I am."

"Good. Up you get then." He nodded his head in the direction of the door behind me.

I swallowed deeply and slowly turned around. Quinn was carrying Stella, walking slowly towards us. I glanced quickly behind her, but there was no sign of El yet.

I gave Quinn a kiss on the cheek, and Stella one on the forehead as they reached us.

I heard the whoosh of the door opening and everything else fell away.

Holy fuck.

I couldn't move, I could barely remember how to breathe.

She was *so* beautiful.

I knew Reeve was walking next to her, leading her down, but I couldn't acknowledge his presence. It was just me standing there, waiting for the most beautiful woman in the world.

Her eyes sparkled, and she gave me a shy smile.

I felt a huge grin break out on my face.

So beautiful.

I felt Logan's hand on my shoulder, but I couldn't look at him either. I wasn't sure I'd ever be able to look away from her. The sight of her made me feel nervous. For the first time since I'd proposed to Ellerslie, I was worried that the words wouldn't come, that nothing I could possibly say would be enough to convey what she meant to me.

I wasn't sure when they got to be right in front of me, but my hand reached out on its own accord to hold Ellerslie's. I couldn't take it anymore; I pulled her against me and lifted her off her feet. She giggled as I swung her around and around. I slid her slowly back down my body so her feet were on the ground once more.

"I'm the luckiest man in the world," I told her simply before claiming her lips.

"I don't think this is the part where you're meant to kiss the bride, cowboy," she whispered, breathless from our kiss.

I chuckled. "Fuck the rules, remember?"

"Lawson Pierce and Ellerslie Rush?" a voice called from behind me.

"That's us," I called back, my eyes still not leaving El's face.

"You're up."

***

All our paperwork checked out, and suddenly it was time to say our vows. I'd kept hold of El's hands throughout the entire ceremony, and now she gestured for me to let go.

I shook my head. "I didn't write anything down," I admitted sheepishly.

Hers eyes widened slightly before an 'of course you didn't' look crept onto her face.

"I knew I wouldn't need to," I reassured her.

"Well by all means..." Amusement danced in her blue eyes.

I took a deep breath and looked deep into her eyes.

"Ellerslie Rush, I'm not sure there are words," I told her honestly. "It struck me earlier, as I watched you walk towards me, that nothing I could say would be enough. Nothing I could say would truly be able to explain the way that I feel for you. The depths of my love for you can't possibly be measured with words."

I squeezed her hands gently.

"I wake up in the morning and my very first thought is of you, I miss you when you leave the room, hell, sometimes I miss you if you're out of my reach. I fall asleep next to you, my mind filled with you, and I couldn't imagine it any other way."

I felt El's hands tremble slightly. I ran my thumb backwards and forwards over the soft skin on the back of her hand.

"My life before you seems like a blur. You taught me what it means to love another person with everything you have – how to truly belong to another. All I hope for this life is to be a good man, a devoted husband and a hell of a father. You came into my life and pierced my heart, and I know I'll never be the same again."

I watched a single tear fall down El's cheek and I let go of one of her hands to gently brush it away. Taking her hand back in mine I smiled at her.

"I love you, El, I think I've been in love with you from the first moment we spoke. You keep me in check, you're smart, you're witty, you're kind and you're generous. And god, you're beautiful... you are *so* beautiful, El, I've never seen someone look as perfect as you do right now."

She blushed, and I chuckled.

"Like I said... no words are enough, but I've decided it doesn't matter. I've got time, shit, I've got forever to show you how much you mean to me and how much love I have for you. You are my present, my future and my forever, Ellerslie."

I took her ring from my pocket, lifted her hand and slid her simple platinum wedding band on. I lifted her hand to my mouth and placed a soft kiss on her knuckles, signaling that I was finished.

El giggled nervously and swiped at the tears pooling in her eyes. I heard Quinn sniffing somewhere behind me.

"You write part time for Hallmark or something?" she whispered, reliving an old joke of ours.

Our small group all laughed at her.

I chuckled deep in my belly. She was nervous – I could tell.

"It's okay, pretty girl. I'll love whatever you say."

She let go of one of my hands and reached behind me to take a sheet of paper and my ring from Quinn.

Breaking tradition, she took my hand and slid my wedding band onto my finger. I smiled at it there, the feel of it heavy and welcome.

"I may not have had a dress ready, or shoes, or anything really," she admitted with a smile. "But I do have this." She indicated to the sheet of paper in her hands.

"This, is the best I could do to explain how you've changed my life, and how much I love you, Lawson."

I nodded at her to go on. She locked her eyes on mine and I shivered under her gaze, I knew she was looking right into the very centre of me.

"Lawson Pierce, you are the one thing I never expected, the one thing I never accounted for in my life. I thought, after living for twenty-seven years that I had a pretty good idea of what it meant to love and be loved in return."

The hand holding her paper shook gently, but she went on.

"But I know now that I had no clue. I had no idea what it was to experience true, pure love. Love like yours. You've shown me that. You love me without limitation, without fear, and without judgment. And not only that, you've taught me how to love you back the same way. I no longer hold fear in my heart. I know there isn't a single thing in this world that you wouldn't do for me if I asked you, and just that knowledge is enough for me."

My chest started to feel tight as I listened to her speak.

She knows... she knows she's my everything.

"What I wanted to tell you, Lawson, is that I know the way you love me, I see it in everything you do and everything you say... and I need you to know that I love you back just as much. No more – even though we joke." She smiled. "And no less. You are my equal, my love... my life. I know what my life is like without you in it, and I also know that it is not a life I'll ever live again."

She stepped towards me and let the sheet of paper fall to the floor. I wrapped my arms around her waist and her arms instinctively draped loosely around my neck.

"I love you, Lawson. I love you now, I'll love you tomorrow, and I'll love you every day after that."

I didn't know if she was finished, and I didn't care. I claimed her mouth with urgency and passion. I kissed her with everything I had, pouring my heart and soul into the moment.

We broke apart at the clearing of a voice. "Well, I guess there is no need to prompt you to kiss the bride."

I chuckled lightly, my forehead resting against El's.

"I now pronounce you husband and wife," he said, humor in his voice.

"Husband and wife, huh, pretty girl?" My heart soared at the use of the word.

She's my wife.

"You're stuck with me forever now, cowboy," El teased.

I'd never been happier about anything in my entire life.

***

We spent the entire night tangled up in one another.

We made love in a way I'd never experienced. It was as though the knowledge we were tied to each other in such a permanent way had sparked an even deeper level of intensity I hadn't known was possible.

El had been so ready, so eager to have me inside her that we hadn't even got her wedding shoes off. I'd looked her up and down afterwards and I couldn't remember seeing anything sexier in my life. There she was, completely naked, just a pair of silver high heels on. The sight alone had been enough to get me hard again. I don't know what had come over me, but she had me wanting more, even when I was so tired I could barely lift my head from the pillow.

She eventually fell asleep first, the sheet wrapped loosely around her beautiful body. I hadn't wanted to disturb her, so I left her that way, draping the covers gently over her and tucking myself in beside her.

I drifted off quickly, her moans still a vivid echo in my ears and her scent thick on my skin.

"Forever is a long, long time, but I wouldn't mind spending it by your side. Tell me, every day, I get to wake up to that smile. I wouldn't mind it at all."
- Author unknown

14. Ellerslie

I smiled as I stopped at the fridge and ran my finger over the photo stuck up with a heavy, black magnet.

It was Lawson and I, on our wedding day. He was holding me in his arms, my feet off the ground, our eyes were focused on each other, the blissful look on my face was mirrored on his. It was a perfect moment – captured on Quinn's cell phone.

I'd just told him he was stuck with me forever, and the look on his face had told me it was something he was more than okay with.

I couldn't believe it had been two months already. We had Stella's things all throughout the house, her room was finally set up just how I wanted it and we'd made space on the walls for some of the artwork from Michael and Cassandra's apartment. We were settled.

Stella entering our lives had been challenging. It was a delicate balancing act between home and work life, and I often found myself thinking that the slightest mishap would totally throw everything out. It hadn't happened yet though, and I knew that despite everything, we were doing pretty well. Lawson and I both had cut down our hours, leaving Quinn and Logan with more responsibility that they were happy to have. Logan had even agreed to become Lawson's business partner and had bought fifty percent of the company just last week.

I straightened the wedding photo. It had been warmer then. I looked outside at the rainy, cold day, and sighed. It would be Christmas soon. I couldn't wait to spend the day with Stella. Having a child in the house made Christmas exciting and magical again. We'd even gone and picked out a giant, live Christmas tree earlier in the week.

I'd been shocked when we got it home, and Lawson announced that it was the first tree he'd ever purchased for himself. I'd made it my mission right then and there to make this the best Christmas any of us had ever had. Stella was going to be spoiled rotten. Not only by us, but by everyone. Quinn, Logan, Reeve and Lisa, and our parents too. I'd joked to Lawson that we might need to do an extension to the house to make space for all the gifts she'd be getting.

Lawson, of course, had taken me almost seriously, and had begun working on the most amazing and extravagant outdoor playhouse I had ever seen. The thing was huge; it was a mini version of our home, although single story, and it even had its own wraparound porch and real glass windows.

Stella was nearly eight months old, and although she was now crawling around at one hundred miles an hour, she was far too young to be using a playhouse. I'd pointed that out to Lawson, but I think he was having too much fun with it to stop now. Even Logan had been coming over to help him build it in the weekends.

Big kids.

"Mamamama," Stella's babbling came from the doorway. I watched in amusement as she scuttled on her hands and knees across the wooden flooring towards me. "Mamamama," she screeched more loudly.

I bent down and scooped her up, blowing a raspberry on her cheek as I did. Stella mimicked me, blowing out and sending spit flying everywhere. I grimaced as I wiped the drops from my face.

Lovely...

I heard Lawson's deep laugh. "You asked for that one, baby."

I tapped Stella on the nose before smiling at him. "I guess I did, huh?"

I popped Stella in her highchair, grabbed a yoghurt from the fridge and set it on the tray in front of her. I didn't bother with a spoon – Stella liked to use them as missiles, and she preferred to eat with her hands anyway.

I was never sure how they knew, but within thirty seconds of Stella being given food, both dogs appeared in the kitchen. They'd quickly learned that if they sat close enough, she would throw them food. She thought it was utterly hilarious to chuck them her dinner rather than eat it herself.

I'd learned, with parenting, some things just weren't worth worrying about, and now I just laughed along with her most of the time.

"Mamamama!" Stella yelled at the top of her voice.

Sippy cup...

I snagged the handle of her cup from the bench and placed that on her tray too. She clapped her yoghurt-covered hands together and sent large drops of it in the direction of the dogs.

I caught Lawson's smirk out the corner of my eye. He was always intrigued by the way I always seemed to know what Stella wanted.

"She's babbling so much now," Lawson commented as he sat down on the seat next to Stella.

I smiled. She was growing up so quickly. I thought back to the first time she babbled 'Mama' at me. I'd held back my freak-out long enough to acknowledge her achievement, and then I'd left the room in tears.

Lawson had given me some time. He'd put Stella down for a nap and then found me hiding in our bedroom.

"What's bothering you, pretty girl?" he'd asked with his arms already open for me.

I'd gotten myself together by that point, but the question had a new wave of tears starting.

"I just feel like a fraud," I'd choked out between sobs.

"What?" Lawson had asked, clearly dismayed.

"I'm not her real mom. She's calling me Mama, and I'm not..." I sobbed loudly. "I just feel so guilty that it's me and not her real mom."

"Hey." Lawson pulled me into his arms. "You *are* her real mom. You do everything for that little girl, and I know how much you love her. That's what a mom is. What happened isn't your fault, El. You're just doing what's best for Stella. And what's best for her now, is you. It's us."

I'd looked up at him through tear-soaked eyelashes and known he was right. Michael and Cassandra weren't here. That couldn't be changed, and it was all up to us now.

Stella snapped me back to the present by doing another loud raspberry and spraying yoghurt all over the newspaper Lawson was trying to read. That was our usual routine, I made the coffee, and Lawson read the paper aloud to me, picking out articles he thought I would like – I didn't care all that much what he read, I just liked the sound of his voice.

Lawson breathed out deeply as he looked at his messy paper. "You really have to stop doing that with her, El." I could hear the amusement in his voice, and I knew he was trying not to laugh.

I looked over at him and exploded into laughter. He had yoghurt all through his hair.

"What?"

"Nothing." I giggled. "I'm just glad you haven't showered yet."

"Stella," he groaned as he ran his hand through his filthy hair.

Stella gave him a toothy grin and shoved her hand back into her yoghurt pot. She had three teeth now, and we'd been given an insight into some of the hard yards of parenting a baby – Stella Pierce did not do teething well.

"Go shower, cowboy, I've got this ratbag under control."

He raised his eyebrows in disbelief. "Yeah... it really looks like it," he teased as he rose from his chair.

I couldn't help but stare at the way his muscles bunched and relaxed as he pushed up and moved away from the table.

He really needs to wear a shirt...

He smirked at me on his way past, he knew me well enough to know exactly what was going through my head.

I sighed as he moved out of my line of sight, his swagger all sexy and alpha male.

"C'mon, Stella, lets clean you up little lady."

***

"What color scheme are you having again?" Quinn asked, her head hidden behind one of the wedding magazines she was reading.

We've been over this...

"I need a color scheme?" I feigned confusion. I was messing with her – I'd picked it out weeks ago when I'd seen just how serious Quinn was about this wedding reception.

She narrowed her eyes at me.

"Silver, white and navy blue." I nudged her knee. "You should know, you chose our dresses."

"Right." Quinn nodded, all business.

Something isn't right with her.

"You need to relax, Q. It's not going to be the end of the world if the tables aren't quite right, or the wrong lace gets delivered, or—"

"It will fucking so," Quinn interrupted me. "It's going to be perfect."

We'd chosen to have a wedding reception to celebrate our marriage. Well in reality, Quinn had decided, and we'd picked New Years Eve to host it. It was going to be in the restaurant Lawson owned. I'd insisted on that. So much had started there for us, and in my mind, it was the perfect place. We had cancelled all the other plans we'd made on our original date, and made donations to the companies that had refused to take a part payment from us.

We had nearly everything organized for the party. I had become close with a few of the teachers from Stella's pre-school and more than one had kindly offered to have her over night for us – so that was one less thing for us to organize.

My girls were coming out from back home, my parents, the twins, Law and Q's mum, aunties, uncles, cousins... everyone was coming to spend the night with us.

"I've given Ricky free range with the food," I told her as I curled a strand of hair around my finger.

Quinn nodded in approval. "Good idea. That man is a genius in the kitchen."

She jotted some notes down in the giant planner she'd started bringing around, and I rolled my eyes.

"What did Lawson say about the decorations we talked about?"

Quinn wanted to have a living wall installed and fitted out with beautiful plants and twinkly lights. I'd thought it was over the top, but when she showed me an image she'd found, I couldn't argue that it looked amazing.

I smiled sweetly at her. "He said I could have whatever I wanted." I giggled as I looked at Quinn's face.

"Don't get me wrong, that's a win for the living wall, but I'm just wondering where my brother's balls went."

I threw a bit of screwed up paper at her. "Don't be talking about my husband like that, thank you, I'll have you know his balls are exactly where they're meant to be."

"La, la, la." Quinn covered her ears as she joked. "Enough about his balls, let's get some real work done on this."

I sighed and glanced at the video baby monitor. Lawson was asleep in the rocking chair, Stella nestled against his chest. She was getting another tooth, and she'd literally thrown her toys out of the cot at nap time. They looked so peaceful together like that.

Quinn interrupted me by tapping the end of her pen loudly on the coffee table in front of her. "Excuse me, Mrs. Pierce, could I have your attention for just one minute?"

Mrs. Pierce... swoon.

"I'll tell you what, Q, you can have all the attention you like... if you talk to me about Colt first," I told her quietly.

She sighed, still staring down at her page.

I waited her out, seeing the internal debate she was having with herself. *C'mon, Q.*

"Okay. What do you want me to say?"

I shrugged. "You tell me what there is to tell."

She dropped her planner down and threw the pen down on top of it. "I don't know, El. I don't know what you want me to tell you. You know I've tried to end it with him."

"Clearly not hard enough..."

"I've tried," she snapped.

"Q... I'm not having a go at you, okay?" I replied quietly. I reached across the table and squeezed her hand. "I just don't like seeing you like this. I know you're not happy."

She shook her head. "I'm not *unhappy*."

"I know."

"But you're right. I'm not all that happy either."

"Why are you still seeing him?"

"I told you, he just seems to have this uncanny ability to remain in my life."

"You stopped seeing him a while back though?" I prompted.

"But yet he's back." She sighed again. "I didn't see him for a whole month, and then bam... he comes by the office. 'Just friends' he tells me. Well one thing leads to another and I find myself right back to the start again. I really don't know how it happens."

"Is his age the only reason you think it won't work?"

She shook her head quickly. "Not at all. I gave up caring about that a long time ago. It's just not quite right. I can't put my finger on it, he's gorgeous, he's my type, he's kind, sweet... and he likes me. I just don't know why it's not clicking for me."

"He's not the one," I told her.

That was the problem. I knew Quinn was getting to the point in her life where she was beginning to want something more than ordinary. I think Lawson and I were partially to blame for that.

"He's not. He should be."

I laughed. "It doesn't work like that, babe."

She giggled. "Yeah... I know. I'll end it after your reception, okay? I can't do it to him before then."

"Okay," I agreed. "Just make sure he knows it's for real this time. He's a nice guy, Q. He needs to move on."

She nodded and picked up her planner again. "Okay, lace or tulle on the center pieces?"

Oh god... help me.

***

Christmas came and went faster than I'd thought possible. My parents had arrived five days before, which was an absolute god send. They adored Stella, and since her pre-school had closed down for the holidays, we needed extra help in the form of babysitters.

Lawson and Logan were flat-out at work, and Quinn and I had our hands equally full. Dad being around was amazing, he'd helped out in the office for a few days while mum stayed home and fussed over Stella non-stop.

The twins had both arrived the day before Christmas Eve, surprising us all. Molly wasn't due in until the afternoon of Christmas Eve, and we hadn't expected Kyle until the early hours of Christmas morning. They'd arranged to meet up overseas and travel back together. It was so good to see them; I hadn't realized just how much I'd missed them until they were standing right in front of me. I'd bawled like a baby.

They'd missed so much in my life, and we had the best time sitting around the fire, having a few drinks and catching up on the past few months. They were fans of Lawson, that was safe to say, and they'd fitted into their new roles as aunty and uncle respectively, with delight.

Stella had taken a real shine to Molly, crawling around after her everywhere she went, and Kyle was also a hot new favorite for attention.

I'd looked around the room, filled with the people I loved more than anything else in the world, and I couldn't remember a time when my life had ever been so rewarding and felt so full.

Lawson had been watching me like a hawk all night, and he'd given my leg a squeeze, no doubt unsure about the emotions I was experiencing.

"Thank you," I'd whispered. "None of this would be complete without you."

He'd stood without a word and raised his beer bottle. Everyone quickly caught on and followed suit.

"To family," he said simply.

"To family," we replied in chorus.

***

Christmas day itself was magical. I'd never experienced anything quite like that day and I wasn't sure I ever would again. It was so complete, so utterly perfect. I'd sat in a room crowded with people that I had nothing but love for, and by the end of the day my cheeks had hurt from smiling so much.

I gave Lawson a cowboy hat. I wasn't sure what my intention for it was when I saw it in the store. It was an expensive bloody hat, and I'd deliberated back and forth about whether or not to buy it.

I eventually decided to get it. If he wouldn't wear it in public then I was willing to bet he'd be my cowboy in private. I shouldn't have worried about it. Lawson had opened it and his mouth had turned up in a huge grin. He'd put it straight on his head, walked towards me and dipped me down, kissing me passionately.

"You like it then?" I remembered asking when I finally caught my breath.

"Now I can really be your cowboy," he'd replied with an unmistakable sparkle in his eye.

All of a sudden, I hadn't been able to wait for bed time.

Lawson had given me a wooden photo frame he'd crafted with his hands. Inside it sat a photo of Quinn, Reeve, Lawson and I on that very first night at his restaurant. I wasn't sure I could even recall a picture being taken, but there it was. We were seated in the booth, Quinn and I opposite each other, Reeve next to me and Lawson across from him. Quinn was reaching across the table, lightly squeezing my arm, and we were laughing together about something I couldn't remember. Reeve was sipping on a bottle of beer; his eyes looking in our direction, a smile playing on the corners of his mouth. And Lawson... he was staring at me with an intensity I couldn't even begin to describe. He was like a man seeing the sun for the first time.

I'd told him as much, and he'd just smiled and nodded his head in agreement. "That's because I was."

***

"The sooner you admit it the better, baby." Lawson chuckled, a shit eating grin on his face.

"Okay, fine," I conceded. "The play house was a great idea."

I had been right on the money when I'd said that Stella would be spoilt rotten. But even I had underestimated just what our families were capable of. Stella had been given a wooden rocking horse, a dolls house, a ride-on tractor, a tricycle, a play kitchen, complete with table and chairs, and even a blow up ball pit. And those were just the big items; there were books, blocks, clothes, shoes... if you could name it, Stella now owned it.

Lawson and I had given her a simple handmade bird mobile that I'd seen at a local craft market, and of course her play house. We'd also picked out a pretty antique rose-gold locket that was going to be put away for her to have when she turned twenty-one years old. I'd placed a small picture of Michael and Cassandra holding Stella on one side, and a photo of Lawson, Stella and I sat opposite it. I hoped it would be something she would cherish one day.

I was glad we hadn't gone overboard like everyone else. There literally wasn't space in here for all this stuff.

"I knew it," Lawson teased as we carried the play kitchen, table and chairs, and a variety of other things out to the play house at the back of the house.

"God this is a lot of stuff," I panted as I maneuvered the dollhouse through the door of the play house.

Lawson swiftly took it from me and easily slipped it through the door.

"Stupid big muscles," I grumbled to myself as I ducked in the door frame. I gasped as Lawson pressed me up against the wall, the ceiling only an inch above his head.

"What was that, baby?" He breathed, deep and husky against my ear before trailing kisses over the skin just below.

Oh god...

I shuddered under his touch. "Nothing," I murmured.

"Are you sure?" he taunted, still kissing my skin, his stubble lightly scraping and tickling in a delicious way. "I thought I heard you call my muscles stupid?"

"These?" I gripped his biceps and felt the thick strong muscles flex. "Don't be ridiculous," I panted, his mouth making me feel lightheaded and breathless.

He pulled back suddenly and stepped away from me. "Oh, well, my mistake then." He ducked out of the low door, and I watched in disbelief as he made his way across the lawn, heading towards the porch.

Like hell...

"Oh no you don't, cowboy!" I yelled before taking off after him, full sprint. He looked over his shoulder and saw me coming, turning the moment before I lunged at him. He caught me effortlessly and held me tight against his chest.

"What's the matter, baby?" he asked innocently. I could see the hint of a grin in the corners of his mouth.

"Shut up, you smug little shit."

He chuckled and opened his mouth. I already knew he was going to crack a joke about being anything but little, so I stopped him. I kissed him in a way that always led to clothes being ripped off, furniture being bumped into, toes being curled...

"Fuck," he moaned against my mouth.

"What's the matter, baby?" I teased.

"What's the matter?" he growled. "How about the fact that you've got me so worked up I want to fuck you right now and I can't, because our entire family is inside that house."

His words had me squirming. "You started it," I accused, humor evident in my voice.

He shook his head, a massive grin on his face. "I'm completely out of my depth here aren't I, pretty girl?"

I laughed and mimicked his earlier smack talk. "The sooner you admit it the better, baby."

"I am nothing special, of this I am sure. I am a common man with common thoughts and I've led a common life. There are no monuments dedicated to me and my name will soon be forgotten, but I've loved another with all my heart and soul, and to me, that has always been enough.
- Nicholas Sparks

15. Lawson

I snuck out of bed to get Stella up before she woke El. Today would be a massive day for her and she could do with a sleep in. I was lucky; all I had to do was shower and put on my tux. El, on the other hand, was willingly subjecting herself to a hell of a lot more than that, not that she needed any of it anyway.

Stella shrieked when she spotted me through the bars of her cot. She loved standing up against the sides and shaking the crap out of the thing. I chuckled to myself as she started doing exactly that, her excitement was infectious.

"Good morning, baby girl."

"Dadada... da!" she cried.

I scooped her out of her cot and carried her down stairs. I sat her down on her play mat and she watched me stoke the fire up so it was roaring again.

"Well, I guess we better change that stinky butt of yours, right?"

She squirmed and fought me as I changed her nappy. I still had no idea how El made it look so easy.

Becoming an overnight dad had been a shock to the system, even though Stella slept well at nights, everything was still different. Gone were the days of lying around on the couch watching a movie on a lazy Sunday afternoon. We'd tried that just the other week, and twenty minutes into the movie, Stella had woken from her nap, screaming bloody murder. I still had no idea what happened in the rest of that movie, we'd never got back to it.

Grocery shops were like a race now, we'd figured out that Stella tolerated it for exactly thirty-five minutes before she started grizzling and moaning to get down and crawl. I suggested once that we let her crawl around the store, but the look on Ellerslie's face had told me that it wasn't such a great idea.

All in all, we were doing pretty well. Neither of us really had a clue about what to do, but, like all new parents, we were figuring it out as we went.

Stella was happy. That was the most important thing.

***

"Is this the part where I call a stripper and we get you shit faced? Make up for you being a pussy and bowing out of having a bachelor party?" Roman's booming voice filled the room.

I just chuckled and took another swig of my beer. He'd been laying the guilt on thick all day.

"No strippers," Logan piped in. "He's a married man now. Let's just get him wasted."

"El would have his balls." Josh smiled a shit-eating grin as he taunted me.

I shook my head at my so-called friends. "She'd have all your balls actually. And I'd buy her a nice handbag to carry them around in, you bastards."

Roman barked out a laugh.

I pointed at him. "Just wait until it's your turn, man, I'll remember this."

"Nah... no woman is that stupid," Josh goaded Rome. It worked too; Rome lunged for him just as Josh darted out of his reach.

"Now, boys... let's not do anything silly."

I turned at the sound of Q's voice and found her standing just inside the door, already dressed and ready.

"Jesus, Pierce, you look good." Rome added a wolf whistle as he looked my sister up and down like a drooling dog.

Quinn rolled her eyes. "Charming as always, Roman."

"Seriously though, what have I gotta do to get a piece of that a—"

"I'm not afraid to knock your head in... even wearing this tux," I interrupted him.

Rome just laughed. He was always trying to rattle me.

"Give the guy one day off from your shit, would you? It's practically his wedding day," Josh joked with Rome.

I shook my head.

I don't know why I do this to myself.

"You look beautiful, Quinn," I told her.

"Thanks, those professionals can work wonders."

Quinn, El, Brooke, Stacey and Jemma had all been getting styled and plucked and painted and god knows what else upstairs, a team of hair stylists and makeup artists had been up there for hours. Lexie wasn't able to make it, and even though El was crushed, she understood – Lexie had her dream job, it was demanding, but she loved it and she couldn't risk upsetting things by asking for the busy season off.

It was just the nine of us here. Even Stella and the dogs were out for the night. Kaylie had picked Stella up a few hours ago, and she'd been more than happy to go with her favorite teacher.

Ellerslie's parents were staying with Reeve, and my mom was staying at Q and Logan's place. All our other family members had rented hotel rooms close to the restaurant for the night. I'd offered for them to stay here, since the place would be empty. I had plans to surprise El with a sweet little bed and breakfast for the night. I'd organized for us to be driven there after the party tonight. I'd sworn everyone to secrecy; I hadn't wanted to risk El finding out about it.

"Anyway, I've come for a reason. We've decided she needs a grand entrance. Can you come and wait at the bottom of the stairs?" Quinn asked.

I couldn't explain the butterflies I felt racing around in my stomach. We were already married for Christ's sake. I'd seen her in her dress, I knew how beautiful she'd look, but the nerves didn't fade as I nodded and followed Q to the bottom of the staircase.

"I'll be right back," she called over her shoulder as she raced upstairs.

I felt the guys crowd around me.

"I'm not sure you three need to greet my wife with me," I joked.

"Are you kidding?" Rome shoved me with his shoulder. "She might see me first and realize she's made the wrong choice."

I glanced at Rome who was wearing a massive, smartass grin.

"You are such a moron," Josh muttered. "They're already married." He shook his head, unable to believe the stupidity of our friend.

"You're a moron too, if you think that's the only problem with his scenario." Logan chuckled. "That girl won't even see us standing here."

I barely registered their jibes backwards and forwards. I heard the click of the photographer's camera, and I knew El was on her way down.

The girls descended one by one, Jemma first, followed by Stacey, then Brooke and finally Quinn. They were all wearing navy blue to match Quinn, but they each had chosen a different style of dress.

They all looked beautiful, which of course Rome told them, in his usual tactless manner.

Guy has always got his mouth open...

He fell silent the moment El appeared at the top of the platform. Her long blonde curls were smooth and silky, tamed and pinned to the side with the lengths over her shoulder. She had on more makeup than I was used to seeing, and her skin was almost glowing.

I tried to swallow, my throat suddenly feeling dry.

Logan was right. She only saw me.

It gave me chills.

I looked into her eyes and she froze, both of us staring at one another, drinking each other in. We stayed like that, unmoving, for what felt like forever.

I looked at the distance between us and knew there was no fucking way I could wait that long to feel the warmth of her body against mine.

I looked at her again and stepped forward. Her mouth curled up into a smile. She knew I was coming for her.

I held her gaze as I climbed the stairs, stopping only when I was one step below her, our faces level.

"You look so handsome," she whispered, running her fingers gently through my hair, pushing it back from my face. "So handsome," she murmured again as her finger lightly traced the planes of my face.

I could hear the photographer clicking away like crazy, but there wasn't anything that could make me turn away from her in this moment.

I opened my mouth to speak but nothing came out. She literally had me speechless. I shook my head and tried again... nothing.

She giggled at my reaction and leaned into my body. "Thank you," she whispered in my ear.

"I didn't even say anything," I finally choked out.

"I know," she replied quietly. "You couldn't... so thank you, for the compliment."

***

Quinn and El had done an amazing job in here. The restaurant was almost unrecognizable, and the night was flowing without a hitch.

We'd had the speeches, I'd kept mine what I thought was reasonably simple, but when I'd looked up, there wasn't a female in the house with dry eyes. Logan had given a heartfelt speech, wishing El and I all the love in the world, and

Rome and Logan had taken the piss out of me and attempted to hit on my wife. So, all in all, it went well.

Quinn had spoken beautifully on behalf of the girls and had El in tears before she even finished speaking. Those two were more like sisters than friends and it warmed my heart to witness the bond they shared.

El's father had even spoken, welcoming me warmly to their family – a sentiment that was both unexpected and incredibly humbling.

I reached for El's hand under the table. "It's nearly time, pretty girl."

I was nervous as shit. El thought I was worried about dancing in front of everyone. She'd managed to twist my arm, and we'd taken a few lessons since we were officially married. I knew how to move, but ballroom had never been my style. It turned out to actually be pretty easy, but I'd let El think that I wasn't feeling confident about it.

"I know." Her eyes sparkled.

I knew she was excited. We'd chosen to dedicate a song to one another. El's choice was up first.

"What have you got for me, Els?" I stood and held a hand out for her.

"Let's find out, shall we?" She smiled shyly.

Quinn, seeing us heading to the makeshift dance floor we'd set up at the restaurant, grabbed the microphone. "Excuse me everyone, it's time for the first dance. If I could introduce to you, Mr. and Mrs. Pierce."

The crowd cheered around us and El blushed, still not thrilled about being the center of attention.

I took her in my arms and held her close as the music began to fill the room.

I listened carefully, not wanting to miss a word of the gift she was giving me. I smiled as I recognized the song. 'The Book of Love' by Gavin James.

"I love you, Lawson."

I kissed her softly and held her tight against my chest, swaying and moving only slightly – the dance lessons forgotten. Thankfully El didn't seem to mind.

I almost laughed at the irony of the words. El was in for a surprise.

"It was perfect, pretty girl," I whispered as the song came to an end.

"Did you like it?" she asked nervously.

"I loved it."

I looked away from El and caught Q's eye. I gave her a nod and she jiggled with excitement.

I loosened myself from El's arms. "I've got a surprise for you."

Quinn and the girls appeared behind El and pulled her gently backwards. I could see the confusion on her face, and I just chuckled. I ran my hand through my hair, my nerves suddenly front and center again.

The minute I saw that El's eyes were covered by the blindfold, I turned, looking for Logan. He emerged through the crowd of our family and friends, passing me a chair and my guitar – the one and only secret I'd ever intentionally kept from Ellerslie.

Quinn pushed down gently on El's shoulders until she was sitting on a seat in the middle of the dance floor. I quietly placed my chair in front of her as the boys joined El's friends. I gave them a nod – I'd asked for their help on this one and I was hoping like hell they'd been practicing.

Q loosened El's blindfold and it fell into her lap. She blinked twice, and her mouth fell open in shock as she realized what was happening.

I lightly strummed the guitar.

Show time.

16. Ellerslie

No way... no fucking way.

He couldn't play the guitar... could he?

He strummed once and behind me I heard a group clap in unison.

The girls? The guys?

I couldn't take my eyes off Lawson to check. I had no choice, I was completely fixated on him. He hummed lightly to the tune.

The strums of his guitar and their timed claps created a chilling melody that I recognized instantly. 'Work Song' by Hozier. I loved this song.

The whole room was silent as Lawson opened his mouth.

His voice was deep, but somehow soft as he sang into the microphone in front of him. His eyes were focused on mine, and I had goosebumps covering my skin from his intensity. His voice moved through my entire body, his foot tapping to the beat he created.

I'd heard him sing before. He was always singing softly to me and Stella, which was part of the reason I'd chosen the song I had. But I'd never heard him sing like this. If I was honest, I didn't know he had it in him. I found myself wondering if there was a single thing in the world that this man couldn't do.

His eyes left mine only momentarily to close when he found himself particularly caught up in a verse, his head lifting slightly to the ceiling. The moment he opened them again, they were focused on me.

I'd never experienced something so chilling, so intense, yet so romantic. The strums of his guitar and the claps behind me were all that filled the room until they slowed and stopped altogether.

The room remained silent for a fraction of a second, and it was only then that I realized I was crying. Cheers erupted from every angle, and I laughed, a snotty, mess of a laugh. It was all so surreal.

Lawson had barely looked away from me, and he didn't now either, he slid his guitar to the side, crouched on the floor in front of me and took my hands in his.

"I love you, Ellerslie."

I could do nothing other than cry and laugh.

***

My feet ached from all the dancing. I'd ditched my shoes two songs in, as had most of the girls. I'd danced with Lawson the entire time. I knew it was our wedding reception and we were supposed to be mingling with our guests, but I just didn't give a shit. The feel of his hard, strong body moving in sync with mine had always been one of my favorite things, and it was my wedding, so I was doing what I wanted.

Quinn had eventually come over and dragged me away to get a drink with her.

"Did you know he could do that?" she asked, her green eyes wide and excited.

I shook my head. I couldn't hide the goofy grin on my face. "I've heard him sing before, not *really* sing like that, but enough to know he had an amazing voice. But the guitar was a complete shock. I really had no idea he played."

Quinn smiled triumphantly. "I told him to keep it a secret, right back after you first met."

I narrowed my eyes at her. "I don't get it? Why hide it?"

"Because," she said, inclining her head in the direction of the dance floor. "When I saw how he felt about you, I knew he'd need a trump card sooner or later. And when you sat there in that chair, he finally got to throw down."

"You had us married off before we'd even kissed." I remembered fondly.

"Well, I was right, wasn't I?" she teased.

"Yeah." I nodded and squeezed her hand. "I've never been so happy to prove you right."

17. Lawson

"Well shit, Pierce, credit where credit's due." Josh pulled me in for a hug and a smack on the back. "I've never heard you sing like that."

I shrugged. "It wasn't a big deal."

"Oh hey, don't go getting all modest now." Rome chuckled, his voice louder than usual.

I shook my head and laughed. "You're a pain in my ass, you know that?"

He gave me a shit-eating grin and held his fist out to me. I bumped mine against his and waited for the questions that were sure to come.

"So, where'd you learn to do that?"

I took a swig of my beer and smirked at him, not wanting to answer.

Rome raised an eyebrow at Logan in question. Logan was my oldest friend, and probably the only person outside of my family to hear me sing, until today anyway. If anyone was going to have the answers it was Logan, and Rome knew it.

"He's played and sang like that since he was sixteen years old," Logan told him, sounding almost proud.

"So that's how you always got the girls?" Rome taunted me.

Bastard can't even give me a break at my own wedding.

I pushed up off my stool and looked around for El. I stopped and rested a hand on Rome's shoulder. "I didn't even need that, man, my charms and rugged good looks were enough to seal the deal."

I dodged the punch he threw at my shoulder and laughed loudly.

Now... where is my wife...

I found El at the bar and smiled to myself. I leaned in and asked Jackie, my bar manager, to get me two tequila shots.

I prowled towards her. "Here you go, pretty girl."

"Ugh," she groaned. "What is it with you and tequila shots?"

I chuckled and set it down on the bar in front of her, the lemon slices and salt next to them.

"I think you'll find that you started this particular tradition."

"I didn't realize it was going to become a regular occurrence," she protested.

I raised my eyebrows and waited.

She pouted.

"Marriage has made you tame. What was it you told him? 'Live a little', if I remember correctly?" Quinn teased before heading back to the dance floor, leaving us alone in a room filled with people.

El frowned after her and picked up the shot glass, holding it up to me.

"To amazing memories," I told her, repeating our toast from an earlier time.

She smiled in recognition and crinkled her nose. She clinked her glass against mine. "And to making more," she replied.

***

The fact that it was New Years Eve wasn't lost on our guests, and we counted down to the beginning of a new year in traditional fashion. I hadn't been so eager to share a new year's kiss since I was a hormone-driven teenager.

I released Ells only to dance with my mom.

"You know how proud I am of you?" she said as we swayed slowly from side to side.

She had to strain her neck to look up at me; both Quinn and I had got our height from Michael, and I had to say I was grateful to the man for it; my mom was tiny.

"I know, Mom," I smirked.

She swatted at my shoulder. "No really, you two are so beautiful together. That girl is probably the sweetest thing I've ever met."

"She is." I smiled as I glanced over to where Ellerslie was dancing with Kyle.

"She's changed you, you know that?" she said quietly.

I looked back at my mom, her hazel eyes shining with unshed tears.

"She's made me a better man," I agreed.

"No." She shook her head. "She's made you whole again." She patted my chest as the song slowed and stopped. She reached up to touch my cheek, like she did when I was a little boy. "You were *always* a good man."

"Ever since we met I've known that we're special. That the way we talk and laugh around each other is different than everybody else. That I will never meet anyone I can trust as much as I trust you. And I think most people search their whole lives to find what we've already found."

- Author unknown

18. Ellerslie

My phone rang from where it sat on the seat of the limo next to me.

Lawson had surprised me with a night away from home tonight, it was sweet and thoughtful, and I should have known he would do something like this.

An even bigger surprise had come from Reeve. He, together with my parents had organized us a honeymoon. Quinn and Logan were in on it too, they'd offered to cover for us at work, and my parents would stay at our house to care for Stella and the dogs.

The day after tomorrow, we were heading to Greece for seven days, and I was excited beyond measure. Lawson was shocked; he never expected anything like this from them.

The only problem, in an otherwise flawless evening, had come when Reeve had rushed over to us and explained in hushed tones that he, Lisa, Colt and probably Quinn would be leaving right away. There had been some type of accident, and his business partner, Harrison, Colt's brother, was involved.

That was all I knew. They'd run out an hour or so before midnight, and we hadn't heard from them since.

I picked up the phone.

"Quinn." The relief in my voice was obvious. "What's happening? Is everything okay?"

Quinn must have been in a cab, I could hear the sounds of the vehicle in the background.

"He's okay," she replied quietly. "He'll be okay, but he's pretty hurt right now."

I shot Lawson a glance; he was listening into the conversation. "What happened?"

"We don't know yet."

Quinn didn't sound right, she was quiet. Quinn was never quiet.

"What's wrong, Q?"

"What was it like?" she asked me suddenly, slightly more volume in her voice. "When you first saw him?"

"Saw who?" I asked in confusion.

"Lawson," she answered. "What was it like when you first saw him?"

I huffed out a laugh and squeezed Lawson's leg. "I'm sure you remember. I was so angry, he drove me crazy."

Lawson laughed in the seat next to me and intertwined his fingers with my free hand.

"Yeah, but what was it really like? Did you just... *know*?"

I thought long and hard before answering her. I didn't have a clue why she wanted to know – but I got the sense it was important.

"I'm not sure," I admitted. "I think I knew that I'd never come across someone like him before, and I guess I had a feeling it was never going to end there. I knew there was more to come. He was the most magnetizing person I'd ever met."

I could tell Quinn's silence was a thoughtful one.

"Are you okay?" I asked when it finally got too much for me.

"I'm not sure," she confessed. "Can I sleep on it tonight and talk to you about it tomorrow?"

"Of course," I told her sincerely.

"I love you."

"I love you too," I replied before the line went dead.

"Well... that was... odd." I placed my phone back on the seat and swung my legs to rest over Lawson's. "Did you hear all of that?"

He frowned and ran his hand through his hair. "Yeah I heard it. No idea what to make of it."

"Me either," I agreed, biting down on my lip in thought.

We both sat in silence for a few moments, trying to decipher Quinn's phone call. It was unlike her to be so vague, she was usually upfront to the point of being borderline rude.

"You know Reeve has been worried about Harrison for a while now." Lawson's hand ran gently up and down my arm as he spoke.

"What? Why?" This was news to me.

"Apparently he's always hurt. Bruises, cuts, broken bones... trips to the hospital. It sounds like this time is the worst yet, but still, there must be a link there."

"Maybe he owes someone money?"

"Could be. But I doubt it. He and Reeve would be earning some pretty good cash and I think he owns a nice place."

"What are you thinking then?" I was beginning to realize that he had put some serious thought into this and that he had a theory on the whole thing.

"I thought maybe he'd been fighting. Underground stuff. I reached out to a few contacts a few weeks back, but no one could seem to place him, so that leaves me a bit stumped as to what he's fighting for."

He must have caught the confused look on my face.

"Reeve came to me back before Christmas; he asked me if I knew anyone that might be able to give us some information. He's tried talking to Harrison himself, but he just shuts down and won't talk about any of it." He explained.

"Okay." I nodded. "But the part I'm confused about is why he thought *you* would be able to help."

Lawson looked at me sheepishly. "Well, shit. I thought the guitar was the only surprise I had left up my sleeve." He chuckled nervously.

I raised one eyebrow and waited for him to continue.

"Okay, so remember I once told you I'd been a bit of a scrapper?"

I nodded in acknowledgement.

"Well, when I first moved out here, I fought a lot... mainly for money, in an underground fighting ring." He grimaced, waiting for my reaction.

"Okay," I replied, shocked.

"That's where I met Rome. There were some dodgy dealings going on that I knew nothing about, and if it wasn't for him, I don't think I would have made it out of there alive."

"Okay," I repeated.

"We got to know one another, and we kind of watched each other's backs. It would have only been a matter of time before we had to come up against one another, but thankfully we got out before that happened. The main guys were eventually arrested and put away for a long time. The contacts I still have are pretty decent guys. That's who I called."

"Well...that is... that is quite a story." Images of Lawson beaten and bloody flashed through my mind and I shuddered.

"It was a long time ago."

I surprised myself with my next question. "Do you miss it?"

Lawson's face showed that I'd surprised him too. "Do I miss it?" He rubbed the back of his neck. "I'm not sure. I miss the adrenaline rush, the thrill of a win, but I don't miss the bruises, the pain, the look on the other guy's face when he knew he was losing consciousness... no." He shook his head. "I don't miss it."

Thank god for that.

"Were you good?" I knew the answer to the question before I even asked it.

He chuckled. "Well, Rome will tell you otherwise, but yeah, I was good."

I gave him a questioning look.

"Let's just say, if it came to it, I'm more than capable of keeping you safe," he finally said.

"You were the best, weren't you?" I asked, feeling strangely proud.

He didn't confirm, nor deny, but the way he laughed and tucked me closer into him gave me all the answer I needed.

"Some people cross your path and change your whole direction."
- Author unknown

19. Quinn

New Years Eve.

It had all happened so quickly, one minute I was thinking about how I was going to end things with Colt the following day, the next I was laughing and dancing with the girls and then... *this*.

I'd known something was seriously wrong the moment I'd seen Colt and Reeve's faces. My mind raced, looking for an explanation, but I came up empty. My eyes had scanned the room frantically before finally landing on Ellerslie and Lawson, holding one another tightly, and relief had flooded through me.

"What?" I demanded. "What is it?"

"It's... my brother," Colt choked out.

Reeve grabbed me by the arm and led me swiftly off the dance floor, his other hand on Colt's shoulder, steering him towards the door.

"His brother, Harrison, my business partner, he's been in some kind of accident. He's been admitted into the ICU. We need to get over there right now."

I knew I was being selfish, but I didn't want to go. That was the role of a girlfriend, and I certainly wasn't up for that job.

"I don't think that really includes me, Reeve." I tried to pull my arm from his grip.

He lowered his voice and leaned in closer to me. "Look, I know that you're not going to be around for him forever, but please, Q, he needs someone right now."

His eyes pleaded with me, and I knew I was fighting a losing battle.

"Okay," I whispered, letting myself be led once again.

I thought long and hard in the cab ride to the hospital, I was sandwiched between Lisa and Colt; Reeve was in the front, making small talk with the driver. I thought about how I'd watched El and Law have their first official dance, and I'd just known – known there was more out there for me, and that I was ready to start looking for it.

It was a niggling thought that had been in my mind ever since they'd brought Stella home and settled her into their lives. They had it all, the house, the dogs, and the baby. The revelation that I wanted that for myself too had come as a huge surprise.

"I called ahead, he's on the fourth floor and the ICU is family only, so you'll have to go in and see him Colt, and report back to us when you can. We're allowed to sit outside the room in the waiting area."

I looked at Colt out the corner of my eye. He was the palest I'd ever seen him, and I couldn't recall ever seeing his face without a grin plastered across it. It was unnerving to see him like this.

Turning to me, he reached for my hand, and I let him take it. "Will you come in with me if they'll let you?"

I froze for a fraction of a second before I realized that there was no way they would let non-family members into that room.

"Sure," I agreed. "Whatever I can do to help."

***

It seemed like an eternity that we waited for Colt to come out of the small room. And when he did, he looked worse than when he went in.

Reeve jumped to his feet. "How is he?"

I could see Reeve was barely holding it together, Harrison was his best friend and his business partner, and it was obvious they were very close.

Colt shook his head slowly and sank down into the chair next to Reeve.

"He's stable, but he's beat up pretty bad. Two broken arms, fractured ribs... cuts to his head and legs. He's a mess... they were worried about internal bleeding, but he's been given the all clear on that front."

"He'll be okay?" Lisa asked.

She'd been doing her best to keep us updated, asking favors from the staff members she knew from doing her nursing placement there.

Colt nodded again. "They said he should make a full recovery, they've got him in a drug-induced coma. They said his body just needs to rest because his injuries are pretty bad. They're talking about moving him to the ward some time tomorrow if he comes out of the coma without any problems."

"That's good news, right?" I offered by way of encouragement.

He took my hand again. "Yeah, it could be worse I guess. It was just a shock seeing him like that, you know? He's always been my tough older brother, but the way things have been going lately, I should have guessed we'd end up here."

What is he talking about?

"Do they know what the hell happened to him this time?" Reeve asked.

"The nurses said the police were due to check in on his progress within the hour, so I guess we'll find out more when they get here."

Reeve just nodded, his eyes still fixed on the door to Harrison's room.

Colt noticed too. "I asked, they won't let you in. I'm sorry, man."

"That's okay; I didn't expect to be allowed in there anyway."

"They did let me open the blind in his window though, I'm pretty sure they can't stop you looking in." Colt nodded in the direction of the room.

Reeve jumped to his feet and pulled Lisa up with him. He gave Colt's shoulder a grateful squeeze and with a nod he made his way over to the small window.

"I'm gonna head back in and sit with him. You can take off if you want to."

I gave him a small smile. "I think I might just do that." I squeezed his forearm. "I'm really glad he's going to be okay, Colt."

"Me too. I can call you a cab?"

"Nah." I shook my head. "I'm fine, you go back in, I'll just say bye to Reeve and Lisa."

He stood quickly, clearly anxious to be back in the room next to his brother. He kissed the top of my head, and I tried to convince myself that it was a gesture made between two friends.

I sat for a moment longer, watching his form retreat into the room. I watched as Lisa comforted Reeve, whilst obviously trying to keep her own emotions contained.

Finally, I stood and made my way over to them. I hugged them both and told them I'd check in with them tomorrow.

It wasn't until I turned to leave that my naturally curious nature got the better of me, I glanced into the room and my breath caught in my throat, Colt sat next to the bed, his gaze wary and scared.

But that wasn't what had my heart racing.

It was the man, lying still, clearly unconscious in the bed next to him. He was shirtless and already covered in black and blue bruises. His torso was partially wrapped with a mixture of gauze, bandage and tape. He was a bloodied, broken mess of a man.

His injuries weren't what had me pressing my hands up against the glass panel and straining to get a closer look... it was his face, a face I'd never seen before this moment, but felt like I'd known my entire life.

I'd never experienced the feeling of déjà vu before, but I knew it was happening to me now. It was as though my body, my brain... my soul, recognized him on some deeper level. I was drawn to him in ways I couldn't even begin to explain.

I just knew.

I knew right in that moment that the man lying in that hospital bed held my future in his hands.

Harrison Hunt.

I'd never met the man, I couldn't tell you what his voice sounded like, how he walked, what his sense of humor was like... but I knew him. His soul called to mine and I could feel the point of no return being crossed.

Harrison Hunt.

Harrison Hunt.

My non-boyfriend's older, beaten-half-to-death brother.

Fuck.

I turned and fled.

"Years ago, when I saw you for the first time, you smiled and I asked myself if there is something in this world as beautiful as this smile. Now, when the gold of your hair has turned to silver, and the long road is behind us, I look at you and I think, there is nothing in this world as beautiful as you smiling."
- Author unknown

Epilogue

I couldn't see him, and my hearing had gone to hell, but I still knew he was behind me. My skin still prickled when he was near, even after all these years together.

My love for Lawson Pierce had never wavered. We'd had tough times, everyone did, but the difference was that we came out stronger, we learned from our disagreements, and our relationship blossomed and evolved – we never made the same mistake twice and we listened to one another.

Lawson's love for me was still more solid than the foundations of the house we lived in. We had lived here for over fifty years. Lawson had asked me every year, for so many years, if I wanted to get a new place, something bigger, something smaller, something newer... I'd answered him the same way every year.

"This is our home. I fell in love with you here, we made love for the first time in these rooms, our children were raised here, as were our grandchildren half of the time, and I intend to grow old with you here, sitting in the rocking chairs on the porch. This is our home."

He stopped asking once I'd reached sixty-five years old, sensing that I was, and always would be, content where we were.

Lawson sat down quietly in the rocking chair next to me and I saw him smile at the children running in and out of the playhouse he had built with his own hands so many years ago. They chased one another around and around the garden, scaling the giant apple tree in the orchard at the end of the chase.

"You be careful up there," Lawson called out, as I knew he would – he always did.

The years had made me predictable to him too. As I reached out for his hand, he turned his over, almost at the same moment, waiting for mine to nestle in his.

"Ouch, shit!" A little voice rang out from in the tree.

97

I stifled a laugh.

"That's on you, Ellerslie."

"Me?" I hissed. "Now that's bullshit."

Lawson chuckled deeply. His laugh hadn't changed a bit. "See what I mean?"

I laughed with him and held onto his hand.

"You know, pretty girl…"

I smiled; he'd called me that for as long as I could remember.

"… I think we've done about all we could with this life. I have the most amazing memories."

I looked into his eyes, now surrounded by creases, but still as green as the day I met him.

He ran his thumb lightly over the back of my hand.

"You know what Lawson; I think you just might be right."

Other Titles

Love like Yours Series

Rushed – Book 1
Pierced – Book 2
Hunted – Book 3
Chased – Book 4

Rock Games Novels

Paper, Scissors, Rock: Vol. 1
Hide and Seek: Vol. 2

The Heart Duet

My Heart Needs
My Heart Wants

Acknowledgements

Thank you to all my friends, family and readers for your support and inspiration. Every message, post and comment I've received fuels my fire even more and I have you guys to credit for getting this novella out.

Thank you!

About the Author

NICOLE S. GOODIN is a romance author and mother of two from Taranaki in the North Island of New Zealand.

Mid 2015, she started to write about a group of characters who wouldn't get out of her head. Her first book, Rushed, was published in mid 2016. Her most popular book to date is Paper, Scissors, Rock – a rock star romance.

Nicole enjoys long walks on the beach, pillow fights and braiding her friends' hair. She dislikes clichés, talking about herself in third person, and people who don't understand her sense of humor.

Please feel free to contact her either via her website, email, Instagram, Twitter or on her Facebook page, she would love to hear your feedback. If you're feeling really game, you can even sign up for her newsletter.